There is something about this particular blackbird in the window that concerns him. There is something...wrong...something wrong with this blackbird. From the corner of his eye he sees movement and follows it to the window. The blackbird is still there, still staring at him with those horrible black eyes. What does it want? Those eyes, they...they're so...it's like they can see right through him, and yet there is something undeniably mesmerizing about them. Fearful they're hypnotizing him somehow, he tries to look away but can't. So he studies them harder, staring into the inky pools and allowing them to take him deeper until he sees his own dark reflection in them. And behind him, something else...someone standing in the corner of the bedroom...

House of Rain, originally published 2013 by Darkfuse
Lords of Twilight, originally published 2012, Delirium Books
ISBN: 978-1-948929-30-1

For information address Crossroad Press at 141 Brayden Dr., Hertford, NC 27944
A Mcabre Ink Production - MXvew Ink is an imprint of Crossroad Press.
www.crossroadpress.com

First edition

HOUSE OF RAIN

&

LORDS OF TWILIGHT

NOVELLA DOUBLE SHOT #2

BY GREG F. GIFUNE

CONTENTS

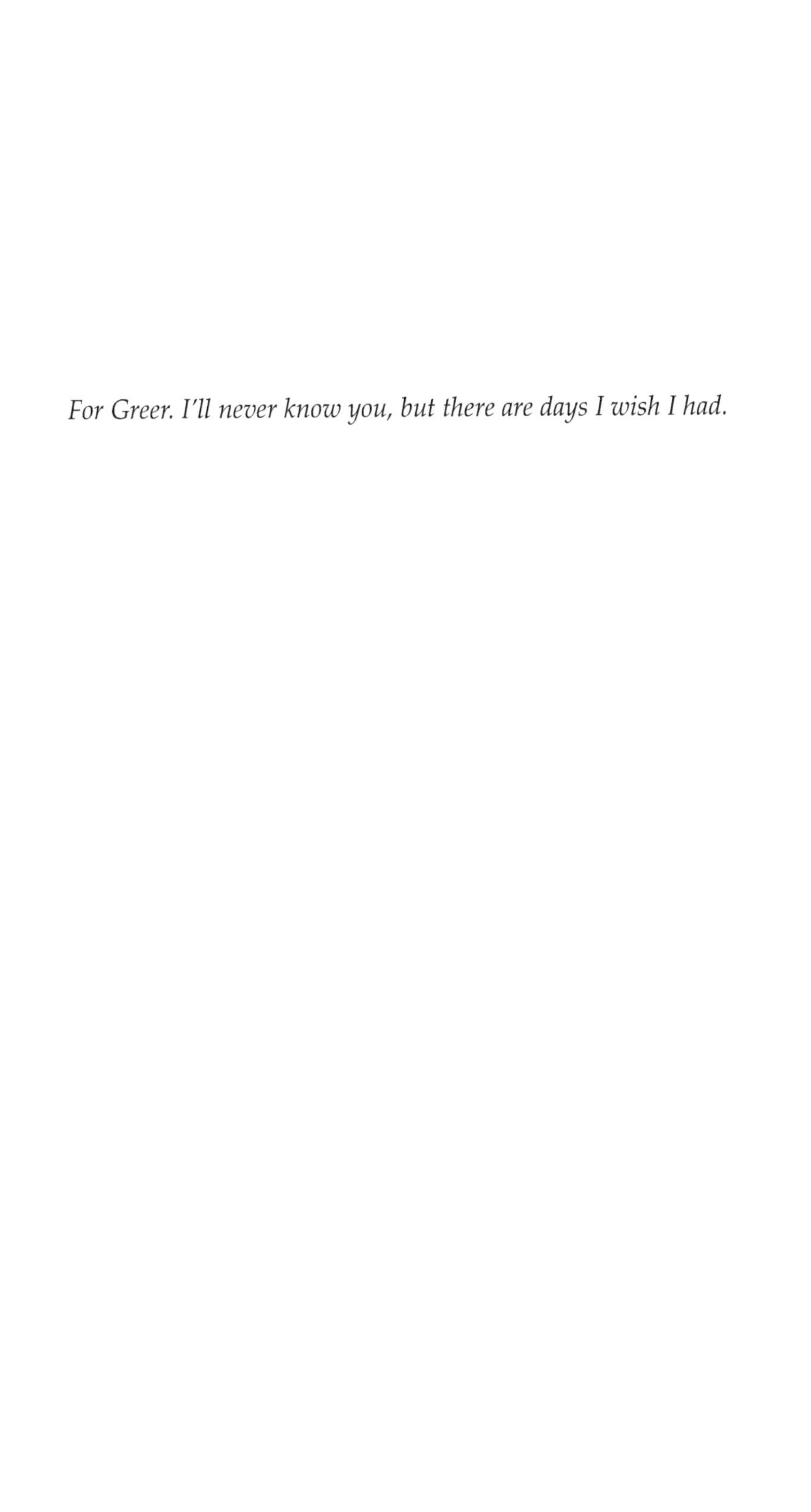

For Greer. I'll never know you, but there are days I wish I had.

"I am still here. Like a spirit roaming the night."
—Son of Sam letter

HOUSE OF RAIN

PROLOGUE

The nightmare had awakened him. Something had been in the room with them, something standing by the window... something not...human. As he lay in bed in the dark, looking at the ceiling, he noticed lights panning across the walls in a rhythmic pattern, sweeping through the room over and over again. As his head cleared, and he slowly became more coherent, he realized they were blue lights.

He rolled over, swung his feet around to the floor and sat there a moment, rubbing his eyes and wrestling a lengthy yawn. With a look back over his shoulder, he saw his wife was still asleep, curled up right next to where he'd just been, her head on the pillow and her body wrapped in blankets. He reached over, gently stroked her cheek with his fingers, then rose from bed and ventured over to the window facing the street.

It had been raining when they'd gone to bed, but now a gentle snow was falling. Three police cars were parked at one end of the block, two more at the other, all with their lights on and all of them positioned in a way so that they effectively blocked off the street at both ends. On the curb sat two men. He couldn't make out much detail, as they were cloaked largely in shadow. One was holding something in his hand, resting it in his lap, and appeared to be staring up at their apartment.

He glanced back over his shoulder. His wife had come awake and had propped herself up on an elbow, her eyes dreamy and still seeing glimpses of sleep. "What's wrong?"

"Not sure."

"I was sleeping so...*soundly*."

There was something wrong about this, but he couldn't put

his finger on exactly what. All he knew for sure was that things he had feared for years, things that he'd put to sleep so very long ago, were coming awake as well.

In him. In her.

"I think the lights woke me," she told him.

"Yeah," he lied, "me too."

ONE

It was raining the night they called about Katy. A hard, primal kind of rain, it pummeled everything in its path and ended up lasting several days. Gordon hadn't seen the weather report, so the rain had been a surprise. But he knew the call was coming, had known for some time, in fact. Not exactly when, of course, but he knew. The doctors had told him it was only a matter of time. But then, isn't everything? He'd always assumed the call would arrive late at night—as those sorts of calls so often do—and that it would roust him from a deep sleep and frighten him awake. He imagined he'd switch on the nightstand lamp and lie there in bed a moment, staring at the phone before finally finding the courage to answer. But it turned out to be nothing like that at all. Instead, it came a short while after he'd finished his dinner. Night had fallen but he was wide-awake and slumped in his recliner with the remote in his lap. An old movie flickered on the television, providing the only light in his small apartment. *The Women,* he remembered, the original, with that great cast of classic actresses. It was one of Katy's favorites. A love of classic movies was something they'd shared, so maybe it was fitting (if not a little eerie) that the call came while he was watching it.

Even before he picked up the cordless handset on the coffee table, he knew what was coming. And somewhere deep inside him, he found the strength to face it. Perhaps he was just exhausted and couldn't take anymore, who could say?

"Mr. Cole, this is Dr. Lynch. I regret to inform you that your wife Katharina passed away just a few moments ago. I'm very sorry for your loss, sir."

Sometimes death is preferable to waiting for its imminent arrival.

Sometimes not.

The memories grow fainter. It is almost over. Night rolled in like always, slow and sensual and dangerous as the dark dreams scraping at the inside of his skull. But the sun is rising now, burning through darkness, illuminating the city, killing night and easing the fear, quieting the whispers of demons and fading his horrible memories to black. Some nights he sleeps, though rarely soundly. Most are spent struggling through long, dark and frightening hours of deceptive silence where the past is still alive and treacherous, its death clutch strong as ever.

Sometimes liquor helps. Drugs always do.

Gordon packs his small glass pipe with weed, sparks it up with a lighter and draws the smoke deep into his lungs. Exhaling, he watches the city beyond his apartment window momentarily vanish in a haze of pot smoke. A warm tingling feeling spreads through him as something akin to relaxation kicks in.

The old devils fade and swirl away into nothing, much like the smoke, yet something of both remains, lingering in the air and trapped within him.

Like a disease, he thinks.

And for Gordon Cole that's exactly what the past is.

In the same recliner, he sits in silence and smokes three consecutive bowls, leaving the room shrouded in a pungent cloud of marijuana. How many hours has he spent in his dreadful piece of secondhand furniture? he wonders. Whatever the tally, he's certain it's too much. When Katy was alive and well, he'd been far less sedentary. Couldn't help but be with such an active woman.

And then, the sickness…

What's wrong, sweetheart?

Not feeling well. Just don't feel right.

So tired all the time, and this cough.

You're awfully pale lately. You'd better make an appointment with the doctor.

Already have. I'm sure it's nothing serious.

Katy's been gone more than a year, but most days it feels like a matter of weeks. Gordon has tried everything. He's read the books about loss and recovery for survivors—even the ones specifically aimed at widowers—he's spoken to the woman from social services and has even seen a psychologist briefly, a soft-spoken middle-aged man named Spires. His office calls now and then to see if he'd like to resume his visits, but he always politely declines and explains he's feeling much better now. They don't believe him—they've no reason to—so they keep calling. Instead, he's begun attending a group meeting for survivors. Run by another psychologist, this one a Japanese-American woman named Amaya, the group meets once a week and has no rules regarding individual participation. Gordon likes this. He's been there twice, but has yet to say anything. No one makes him speak, so he doesn't. He just listens. It seems to help somewhat. Or perhaps it simply distracts him. He can't be sure yet. Maybe he doesn't care.

Gordon closes his eyes. In the darkness, he glides, riding the high, and for just a moment remembers what it is like to be young and strong and agile. He remembers going for a run, or riding his bike. He remembers being alive. And always Katy, his Katy, right there with him, reminding how life can so suddenly become something worth living—something dizzying and magical as any fairy tale—then just as quickly…this.

He opens his eyes, puts the pipe aside and pushes himself to his feet. Shuffling across the den, he slowly makes his way to the kitchen, his worn moccasin slippers scraping the bare wood floors. A chill sets in before he's made it. He's always so goddamn cold these days. Wrapping his cardigan tighter around his pajama top, he finishes his trek to the kitchen. *Christ*, he thinks, *I could spit from one end of this shithole to the other, why do I feel like I just ran a marathon?*

If he listens to the quiet long enough, he can hear Katy answer him.

Because you're an old fart, that's why. Something close to a smile curls his lips. He dismisses it and gets his cereal down from the cupboard. Normally his shoulder is sore, but the pot is a natural painkiller, so he feels nothing. Well, that's not exactly true. Giggling. He feels like giggling, actually. So he does. By the time he's added milk to his Product 19, the laughter has subsided. Strange how he only laughs when he's high as a kite, and even then it's soulless, empty. Meaningless, that's what it is.

Regardless, the giggles return. He is helpless against them.

Damn fool. Stoned out of your gourd at your age.

"Are you on the dope?" he says aloud, using his best authoritarian tone.

Gordon pulls out his chair and sits down at the little table. *Another winner from the Salvation Army store*, he thinks. He sometimes wonders who these things belonged to before, and remembers how one day, while shopping there, a young couple walked by, the man bitching about how he wanted to leave because "all this crap, these clothes and the furniture and whatnot, most of it ended up here because somebody died, you know. You're rummaging through dead peoples' belongings."

Little fucker was right too.

When Katy died and he couldn't maintain the nicer, larger apartment they'd shared for years, he sold or gave nearly everything to the Salvation Army. Now people are sitting on Katy's furniture, using her silverware, even wearing her clothes. And he's doing the same with someone else's things. It gives Gordon the creeps, but he continues to think about such things as he eats his cereal. Here, in this tiny apartment in this less-than-desirable neighborhood, because when Katy died their lives together died too, and with it a huge piece of Gordon.

He finishes his cereal, drops his spoon into the bowl and pushes it aside. The munchies are kicking in. Brownies. He wants some brownies. But he doesn't have any. Why the hell doesn't he have brownies? Can he make some? Would it be worth it to walk down to the convenience store at the corner and get some? Do they even carry brownies? The mix, maybe, but it'll cost a fortune at a place like that. What about those individually wrapped bastards with the nuts? Do they still make those? Maybe pie. He could go for pie, if he can't find a brownie. A fruit pie would be good. One of those Hostess jobs, a blueberry one would—no, wait— cherry—a cherry one. And chips. *Yeah, need some goddamn Pringles in this house.*

Gordon gets up, finds his wallet on the counter. Imitation black leather, it is battered and badly worn. He checks it for cash. Eighteen dollars. He looks to the refrigerator, and the little magnetized calendar on the door, a free one some real estate office sent him and probably everyone else in the city. It's nearly the end of the month. His Social Security check is still a couple weeks away. Wearily, he tosses the wallet and his eighteen dollars back to the counter, and moves across the apartment to his bedroom. The shade is drawn on the only window—since it faces a brick wall it normally is—casting the room into darkness. He switches on a lamp on his bureau, then goes to a small writing desk on the far wall and slides open the drawer. He finds both his checkbook and savings account book beneath some papers. Though he just checked them a few days ago when he paid his monthly bills, he goes through them again anyway. There's two hundred and four dollars in his checkbook, and just shy of five hundred in his savings.

Seventy-two years old, and I have a whopping seven hundred bucks to my name. Christ Almighty. No money for extras this month, no money for those… wait. What did I need the money for again? There was something I wanted to buy but I can't remember what the hell it was. Goddamn pot makes me forget things, I…

His stomach grumbles.

Pies! That's it. Hell, I have more than enough for a couple cherry pies. I can—

A loud crash on the street below distracts him. It's definitely the sound of glass shattering, probably a bottle. Muffled voices come next. Angry, aggressive voices followed by a scream—a man's scream—and then more shouting.

Gordon makes his way back out into the den and looks out the double windows on the front wall facing the street. His apartment is on the second floor, so it's above street level but still close enough to clearly see what's happening below.

A homeless man he's seen numerous times sleeping in the park across the street is stretched out across the sidewalk. Probably a good six or seven years older than Gordon, he is lying on his stomach and looks as if he's fallen and landed there from a great height, his ratty long coat spread out around him on the pavement. Nearby, the shattered remains of a wine bottle lay just beyond his reach. Shards of glass litter his back, and blood leaks from a large gash on the side of his head, forming a halo that trickles over the curb and into the gutter.

Circling him like a pack of banshees is a group of older teenagers, laughing and hopping about, stopping now and then to kick the man in the side. The man attempts to crawl away, but they're on him again, kicking and kicking until he stops moving. People cross the street or hurry past, not wanting to get involved. Cars pass. No one stops.

Gordon recognizes the little punks. They live in the neighborhood, in the projects around the corner. He feels his hands curl into fists as anger rises within him. "Little bastards," he mutters. But he knows he cannot embrace this anger, he must push it back into the darkness where it belongs.

But I should do something, I—do something, for Christ's sake!

"Fucking bum!" one of the kids yells loud enough for it to be heard through the closed window. "Get a job, you begging piece of shit!"

The others laugh and congratulate their friend as the homeless man tries again to crawl away. They allow him to get a few feet away before one of them, the leader apparently, an older boy of perhaps eighteen or so with a baseball cap worn sideways, straddles the fallen man and begins to urinate on him.

A couple of thirtysomething women suddenly appear from the park across the street. One of them is on her cell phone, while the other waves her arms and shouts at the boys, as if this might somehow intimidate them. Instead they laugh, and one of them lunges for her with mock aggression. She stops and stumbles back into the street, where she is nearly hit by a van that swerves, lays on the horn then speeds off. The woman on the phone announces at the top of her lungs that she's called the police and they're on their way.

One of the boys swats the phone from her hand. Another circles behind her and grabs her ass. She spins to slap him, but he's already stumbling back toward his friends, all of them laughing.

Two men join the fracas, one younger and one middle-aged. They step in and protect the homeless man while also positioning themselves between the boys and the two women, one of whom is so angry she has to be restrained from attacking them.

Words are exchanged, threats leveled, and finally the boys move on. As the Good Samaritans check on the homeless man, Gordon steps back from the window. His heart pounds like a hammer in his chest. A bit lightheaded, he returns to his recliner for a moment. He does not close his eyes, because he knows the kinds of visions and memories his brain will summon if he does.

His buzz is nearly gone.

Goddamn neighborhood, he thinks. *Not even safe to go out and buy a fucking pie if I want one.*

"I've got to get out of here," he mumbles. "Go someplace safer."

But no such place exists. Not for Gordon. He knows this.

Katy loved the city, but he's never had much of an affinity for it one way or the other. Why does he stay then? Why once Katy was gone and he could no longer afford to live in a decent neighborhood did he move to this dump? Why didn't he leave when he had the chance? It seemed disloyal at the time. He needed to stay in the city Katy loved. Truth is, he hoped remaining in the city might keep part of her alive for him. He was wrong.

He can hear more commotion and talking outside his window.

Hopefully an ambulance has arrived and someone can help that poor old man.

Old man…

Christ, he thinks, *that could be me out there on the sidewalk covered in blood and piss and God knows what else.*

In the distance, an odd rumbling sounds. It takes Gordon a moment to realize it is thunder he's hearing. He looks to the windows. Rain begins to fall, tapping the panes and gradually blurring the world beyond his windows.

Katy, is that you?

The rain increases, as if in answer.

Or was it only his imagination?

Tell me what to do, sweetheart, I—I don't know what to do anymore, I…I'm so lonely, Katy, I…I'm doomed without you…damned without you…

He despises his weakness. Worse, Katy would not have been too keen on it either. She was the most loving, compassionate, patient and understanding person Gordon has ever known, but she was so strong and practical as well, so no-nonsense. Even she couldn't make this right, but at least she'd have been able to calm him and make the fear subside, if only for a little while.

The phone rings, startling him.

He grabs the handset from the coffee table, the arthritis in his little finger throbbing from the tight fist he made earlier. "Hello?"

"Hello, is this Mr. Cole?" a man with a thick Indian accent asks.

"Yes, this is Gordon Cole."

"Good morning, Mr. Cole, my name is *Andrew* and I'm calling you today from the *American Eagle Vitamin Company.* I would like very much to tell you about a special offer on our multivitamins designed especially for the needs of seniors. We can ship them directly to your door, and just for trying them today and paying with your major credit card, Mr. Cole, I am authorized to offer you free shipping and a special free gift…"

Gordon doesn't want any vitamins and has no intention of purchasing them. But he lets Andrew continue. He even asks questions when he's done, keeping him on the phone as long as possible and pretending that Andrew is a friend who has called to chitchat. It helps him to forget about the homeless man. It helps him to forget about everything.

Finally realizing what he's gotten himself into, Andrew terminates the call.

Gordon hangs up. He glances at the spent pipe and sighs.

The rain keeps falling.

I'm going out there, he thinks. *I'm going out in the rain. I can't stay here anymore. Not in this apartment, not in this city. Maybe not even in this world. I'm going out there and I'm never coming back, not ever.*

But his eyes slowly close, and before he knows it, Gordon is sound asleep.

TWO

This is not a dream. This is real. No matter how hard Gordon wishes it so, this is not something he can force himself to awaken from, because he is not asleep.

In the rain, the city looks like it's melting all around him. A liquid sky lords over distorted reflections in a filthy puddle, ripples and moves in a way only living things can. Living things capable of feeling pain, surface things hiding all that reside and conspire in deeper, darker waters. And through the rain, a premature afternoon darkness begins to swirl, black blood from wounds that will never heal.

Chin tucked, Gordon hurries as best he can through the downpour, hands stuffed in the pockets of his raincoat. The others around him rush about as well, with their briefcases and shopping bags, newspapers and umbrellas, hi-tech gadgets and designer phones. Monkeys in makeup and heels, suits and Father's Day ties, they run for cover across cement plains, seeking shelter in caves and trees of steel and plastic, iron and brick, cages of false security in a facile world of primal fear and delicious madness. Pain and joy, horror and beauty, it's all hidden in plain sight.

An empire of chaos… There, in the rain.

With his demons awakening, coming up out of that long slumber to stagger after him, Gordon crosses over onto a side street, his shoes splashing puddles as he goes. He is short of breath—he can't remember the last time he walked this far without stopping for a while—his legs are sore and his back aches. This damp weather only makes it worse. Every joint aches in wet or cold weather, and this is both, but he is determined to reach his destination without interruption.

The street is narrow, the wet pavement reflecting the dark and dreary buildings lining either side, looming over him like phantoms. Visions flash across his mind's eye, but he ignores them. He must. Otherwise they'll gain power. He hurries over to an awning above the front door of a small bar sandwiched between a condemned four-story walkup and a pawnshop.

Once inside, he feels a burst of hot air. It takes the edge off his chill, but he's still cold, his hands like ice. *Goddamn circulation.* His body slows more and more each day, betraying him little by little. Even his blood is dying, congealing in his veins like molasses. His is a slow death, a free fall into gradual darkness. He shakes the rain from his coat, removes his hat and lets his eyes adjust to the dim lighting. He's been here before, but not for several months. He doesn't recognize the bartender; he must be new, a thirtysomething guy in a sweatshirt and jeans, with a robust build, a shaved head and diamond studs too big to be real in both ears.

"Still coming down pretty good out there, huh?" the bartender says through a wide smile.

Rather than answer such an idiotic question, Gordon orders a black coffee. There are no windows here, and the only light is from small candles encased in red glass along the bar and on each of the tables at the back of the place, which casts everything—even the shadows—in a sinister bloodshot glow.

Gordon sees Harry sitting alone at a table along the back wall and gives him a subtle nod. But for the bartender and them, the place is empty.

After paying for his coffee, Gordon joins his friend at the table. He puts his mug and hat down, then removes his raincoat and puts it over the back of the chair. Wearily, he sits across from Harry and puts a hand on either side of the mug, which helps to warm them.

Harry is Gordon's oldest, dearest friend. He has known him for nearly fifty years, and he is the closest thing Gordon has ever had to a brother. He is the best of Gordon, and also the worst.

"Wasn't sure you'd come," Harry says. Despite fifty-some-odd years in America, he still possesses a slight trace of British accent.

"I told you I'd be here, didn't I?" Harry sips his scotch and soda.

"Coffee this time of day?"

"I'm cold."

"I'm always cold."

"You and me both."

"It's horrible to be old, isn't it?" Harry smiles, flashing long, nicotine-stained teeth, but it's difficult to see much more of him because he remains largely cloaked in shadow. "What I wouldn't give to be able to go back and have another twenty, ten—hell—even five more years of youth."

"Can't live forever, Harry."

"So they say. But then the future's not what it used to be, is it?"

Gordon tastes his coffee. It is strong and harsh and so hot it burns his lips. "Was it ever?"

Harry never answers. After a moment, Gordon tells him about the homeless man who was assaulted outside his apartment earlier.

"The one with the natty beard that lives in the park? He must be ten years older than we are."

"A good five or six, anyway."

"Pukes. They could've killed him."

"They very well may have. He left in an ambulance, I don't know."

Harry runs an arthritically ravaged hand through his thinning silver hair, which he combs straight back and away from his angular face.

"Christ."

"Yeah." Gordon drinks more coffee. Warmth is beginning to return to his extremities. "Just as easily could've been me."

"Or me, Gordo, my neighborhood's no better." He smiles again, but it seems more an expression of pain than joy. "At least you could give them a fight."

"Maybe years ago. Not anymore. I can barely get out of my own way." Harry looks away and to his right, as if he's seen something move across the floor between the nearby tables. "I'm ashamed to say it, but there are days I'm afraid to leave my room."

"Don't be ashamed. There are days I'm afraid too."

Harry downs the rest of his drink, then stifles a belch. "At least there was a time when you *were* tough. Me, I've never liked physical confrontation. I always shied away from it. Stuck to my books and my plays, my paintings. I was never much of a tough guy."

"No one in their right mind enjoys violence, Harry. You were always better than that foolishness, above it."

He stares down into his empty glass. "Maybe I was just scared."

"We're all scared."

"But you were in Vietnam, Gordo, you—"

"I was just a soldier, nothing special. Besides, that was a lifetime ago."

"Not quite that long."

"It was a whole other life, trust me."

Harry sits forward, breaking through the shadows. In his wrinkled trousers, tweed jacket and wool scarf, he could pass for an elderly college professor from a quaint old movie, but his pallid skin bathed in the eerie red glow from the candles gives him an unsettling, almost demonic look. "The point is you experienced it."

"Experienced what?"

"Well, you…*killed* people. Before, in combat, you—"

"Harry, I don't like talking about these things." A pain stabs at Gordon's temple. He winces and pushes his coffee aside. "You know that."

"I'm sorry." He sits back, allows the shadows to better conceal him. "I had no right to…"

Gordon signals the bartender, orders Harry another scotch and soda and one for himself as well. "Look," he says evenly, "you know yourself that when I met Katy that was years behind me, but I was still lost. She changed all that. She washed away all the pain and fear and guilt, and after a while it became something else, something different than memories or the past. In a way, it died."

"Love killed it." Harry raises an eyebrow, pleased with his assessment.

"Yeah," Gordon says. "I guess it did."

The bartender appears with their drinks, offers to run a tab, then leaves them.

Harry raises his glass. "To Katy."

"To Katy."

They click glasses, and drink. Gordon feels badly for Harry. Unlike he and Katy, Harry was married twice, and both ended in divorce. His first wife died a few years ago, and his second wife remarried and has had no contact with him in decades. He has two grown children he hasn't seen in years either, and several grandkids he's never even met. "It's good to see you, Harry. I… needed to see you."

"You too. I was getting worried, hadn't heard from you in a while. At the risk of sounding like the pathetic old fool I am, I'm afraid you're my only friend, Gordon."

"Then we're both pathetic old fools, because you're the only friend I've got too. Except for Katy, you're the only real friend I've ever had."

The two men drink in silence awhile. The bartender sits on a stool reading a paperback novel, a dog-eared copy of Ira Levin's *Rosemary's Baby*. Outside, the rain keeps on. They cannot see it, but they can hear it striking the walls, as if angry it cannot get in.

"Since I lost my Katy," Gordon says hesitantly, "strange things have been happening, Harry."

"Like what?"

"Sometimes at night, when it's very quiet, I'd swear I can hear someone in my bedroom *whispering* to me. But I turn on the light, and no one's there."

"What do they say?"

"My name. Over and over again."

"Do you recognize the voice?"

"No," he says, eyes growing moist. "But I know who it is."

"Nonsense." Harry waves a hand, as if to clear the air between them. "You've got to stop smoking so much pot. You're not a kid anymore."

Somewhere far off in the distance, or perhaps only deep within Gordon's mind, comes the ethereal strain of a saxophone playing a slow, sensual, dreamlike tune. He takes another sip of his drink, then closes his eyes.

White and black balloons falling… people in formal dress celebrating and laughing as champagne flows…and there, across the room…a vision…the most beautiful woman he has ever seen…watching… watching him…before looking away with a coy smile…

He opens his eyes and it's gone, all gone. His hands are shaking. "I'm sorry, Harry. For everything, I…I'm sorry."

"Stop it. You've always been there for me. I was there for you."

Blood sprayed across a cracked bathroom mirror…

"You've been a better friend to me than I ever was to you."

"We all make our own decisions, Gordo. You know that better than most."

"It's been more than forty years, and we've never once discussed that night, Harry. Not once."

Muffled screams echo down a dark corridor…

"Why would we?" Harry fidgets in his chair. "Nothing to discuss. It was a long time ago."

"Sometimes I think the whole thing was just a dream. Do you ever do that?" Gordon looks at him hopefully, helplessly. "Do you ever think it was just a drunken, drug-fueled, hallucinogenic dream?"

"Of course. Doesn't that seem far more reasonable, far more likely?"

"But do you believe it?"

"Doesn't matter. We're old men now. Either way, that clock's ticking. It has been for a very long time, and it's starting to wind down."

"We're just pretending, aren't we?" Gordon asks softly. "There's no way out."

"We're living on borrowed time. But isn't everyone?"

Blood…so much blood…

Gordon wipes his eyes and finishes his drink. The visions fade but his hands continue to tremble. "Think this rain's going to stop anytime soon?"

Harry leans back into the thick crimson shadows. He never gives an answer.

But Gordon knows he has one.

THREE

Somewhere nearby, a phone is ringing. An old rotary phone with a bell-type ring, it is there but very faint, very far away. It rings forever, it seems, and no one ever answers. Perhaps no one can hear it but him.

Blood. There's so much blood. Everywhere. On the floor and the walls, on the ceiling, on the windows. How can there be this much blood? It hardly seems possible. But it is. His nude body is spattered with it, his hair stained and clumped with it, and his hands coated and dripping with it, looking like he plunged them into a can of dark red paint.

As the ringing fades to silence, a whisper slips free of the darkness. "Gordon..." Beyond the blood-spattered windows, the city waits. Unseen things perch on rooftops and hide in alleyways, crouch atop parked cars and watch from the gutters. He knows this now. He can feel them. The veil has become transparent. But soon all these things will return to the world unseen, to the shadows, and they will no longer be his concern. Not anymore. Not for now...

A horrifying scream shatters the silence. And then...tears...great heaving sobs of agony and pain, of realization...

"Gordon..."

"What have I done?" Another scream, this one his own. "God in Heaven, what have I done?"

The phone again begins to ring, swallowing the cries and dragging them back to the impenetrable darkness from which they came...

"Gordon?" Katy's voice now, not a whisper like the other but very soft, very faint... "Are you all right?"

The visions bend and ripple like water, slowly fade and reveal the street and a hard, steady rain. Gordon stands huddled in a deep doorway to an abandoned building, taking shelter under the overhang. Water gushes from the roof above, splashing the pavement with a loud slapping sound and blurring the street and buildings beyond. He focuses, remembers where he is.

There is another sound, just barely audible above the rain. Singing… music…

Across the street, a run-down but functional building that was once a warehouse has been converted into a makeshift church. As if for his benefit, two large barnlike front doors swing open, revealing the interior of the church. Gordon remains where he is and watches a moment. An old woman emerges, her head covered with a plastic kerchief tied under her chin. Clutching her handbag tight, she slogs through the rain and hobbles off down the street.

The congregation is small, and appears to consist primarily of senior citizens and street people, but they are all quite jubilant, dancing and singing a high-octane gospel tune. The preacher, a round little man with a Larry Fine hairdo and a powder blue leisure suit, prances about on a small riser. An enormous wooden cross hangs on the wall behind him, and there is a podium nearby, but he seems oblivious. His is a dance of total abandon. *Overcome with the spirit*, Gordon's mother used to call it when he was a child. Gordon prefers *Bad Theater.* Religion gives him the creeps, but he continues to listen and watch the festivities anyway, at once repelled and strangely drawn to them.

The famous quote from Sophocles, in *Oedipus Rex*, comes to him just then…

"Alas, how terrible is wisdom when it brings no profit to the man that's wise! This I knew well, but had forgotten it, else I would not have come here."

Something in the corner of his eye catches his attention. Afraid of what he might find there, Gordon very slowly looks to the right, away from the church and to the far corner at the end of the block.

The old woman in the plastic kerchief stands in the rain, watching him. He cannot make out her eyes or facial expression, and she never says a word. Even if she does, between the distance, rain and raucous church service, he wouldn't hear her anyway. But she speaks to him nonetheless.

He can hear it in his mind, feel it to the depths of his being.

I see you…I see what walks with you…beside you…within you…

Gordon steps through the curtain of rainwater rolling off the roof, turns and hurries off in the opposite direction. The gospel singing—dizzying and growing in intensity—chases after him, until he reaches the corner and slips into a nearby alley.

Then, there is only the rain.

The far end of the alley empties onto another narrow avenue consisting of mostly abandoned, condemned and fire-gutted buildings. One of the few still in use occupies the community center he's come looking for. He is still in neither a good nor particularly safe neighborhood, but this is where his group meets, and he plans to be gone from the area well before nightfall.

Just as Gordon reaches for one of the large double doors, the wind picks up, blowing trash and debris about along the street. One gust slams into his back with such force it nearly causes him to lose his balance, but he manages to get inside without falling. Leaning back against the door, Gordon takes a moment to catch his breath. Before him is a long and dimly lit corridor, the floor a cheap and badly worn industrial tile, the walls a faded beige and the ceiling fitted with occasional small light fixtures dulled by age and filth. His legs ache, his back hurts and his lungs burn each time he takes a breath. *Too much*, he thinks, *I'm doing too much without resting.* Shaking the rain from his coat, he pushes off and away from the door and follows the corridor down past several offices and meeting rooms, the doors closed. Usually this run-down state services building, which was once, many years ago, a public elementary school, is drab and gloomy, but on this day it seems as if there's something more here. Something…else.

Gordon has never before felt fear here. Today he does.

Still, he continues down the corridor, passing two more closed doors before reaching the meeting room. Normally open prior to the meeting, its door stands closed as well. Gordon checks his wristwatch and finds he's roughly five minutes late.

For a moment he contemplates leaving, skipping it altogether. What the hell is he even doing here anyway?

Hiding…

Still breathing heavily, Gordon looks back over his shoulder at the section of corridor from which he came. More shadows… moving… gliding…spiraling like dark tendrils of smoke. His knees tremble. Is there something there, just beyond the edges of dull light at the far end of the hallway?

"Gordon…"

He wipes rain from his face and squints, but his eyes aren't what they used to be, and he can't make out much of anything. *Because there's nothing there*, he assures himself, *nothing there to see.*

But he's not so sure.

Gordon hears someone talking on the other side of the door. It distracts him just enough to draw him back. He does his best to focus on that instead. Still, he checks over his shoulder one last time, unable to shake the feeling that something is coming, creeping down that corridor, slithering closer each time he looks away. A chill tickles his neck, sending a shiver through his entire body.

Trading one fear for another, he pushes open the door and steps into the meeting room.

Laughter…horrible mocking laughter…

What have I done?

And the blood, as if in answer, the horrible sound of a lifeless body collapsing and slapping against the floor with sickening force…

You lied to me you lied to me you lied to me you—

"Of course…" This isn't real!

"Is the blood real? Is your pain?" You. Are. Not. Real. I didn't do this.

Thoughts—they were only thoughts I— "But I can hear your thoughts. Even now, I can hear your pathetic, whimpering little thoughts, your attempts to explain it even to yourself in the hopes that maybe—just maybe—you can set yourself free. But there is no freedom for you. There is only slavery. Your *slavery…"*

"Gordon?"

Nightmares recede, give way to a large open area with a circle of old metal folding chairs in the center. A converted teachers' lounge, along the left-hand wall are some cabinets, a sink, a counter outfitted with a coffee machine, a stack of Styrofoam cups, plastic spoons, a sugar dispenser and some napkins, and a refrigerator, while the back wall consists almost entirely of large rectangular windows of wire-encased glass. Amaya Adams rises from her chair and starts across the room toward him, the heels of her pumps clicking along the tile floor. Her short dark hair, exotic beauty and petite figure harness Gordon's attention immediately. In a blue, pinstripe skirt-suit, at first glance she looks more like a corporate executive than the psychologist he knows her to be.

"Gordon," she says again, her voice smooth and pleasant, "I'm *so* glad you could join us today. As you can see we have a smaller turnout than usual, likely due to the storm, but please, come and join us." When she is closer, she speaks to him again, this time more quietly. "Are you all right? The way you came into the room, you seem a little…troubled."

"I'm fine," he tells her, forcing a quick smile.

She smiles back. Hers is wider, brighter. "Come in then, join us."

As he follows her across the room, Gordon realizes only three of the chairs are occupied, rather than the usual ten. He recognizes the three group members from his previous times here, but can only recall one of their names—Wayne—the youngest of the group, a red-haired man in his thirties. Gordon only remembers this because Wayne often refers to himself in the third person and because Gordon finds him relentlessly annoying.

"You all remember Gordon,"

Amaya says cheerily, motioning to the others. "And Gordon, you remember Wayne, Jerry and Robert."

Jerry and Robert. Right.

"What's up?" Wayne says. Tall, in relatively good shape and dressed in his usual sweat suit and sneakers combo, he reminds Gordon of a gym teacher or a coach of some kind.

"Believe that rain?"

"Hi Gordon," Jerry says. An overweight man in his sixties, he has a penchant for flowered shirts and sandals with socks. His wavy salt-and-pepper hair is quite disheveled, he could use a shave, and his smile reveals crooked, unkempt teeth.

Robert, an African-American man a bit older than Gordon, gives a less-than-enthusiastic wave but says nothing. Bald, with a neatly trimmed mustache and thick glasses, he is dressed casually but impeccably, and seems somewhat dismayed by the interruption.

Gordon nods to each in turn, then removes his hat and coat and drops into the chair farthest from everyone. He looks back at the door. It remains closed.

"Robert was just sharing a story," Amaya explains, returning to her seat.

"Why don't you go ahead, Robert?"

"I was talking about the evening hours," he says, looking at Gordon, "and how difficult they are for me. The evenings are so empty without her. It's when I feel the most alone."

Gordon nods but offers no reply. "Are your evenings generally quiet, Robert?" Amaya asks.

"My entire life is quiet," he answers. "So quiet it's deafening sometimes."

"That doesn't even make any sense," Wayne says, but he laughs lightly when he says it. "How can it—"

"I didn't mean it *literally*," Robert tells him crossly. "For God's sake."

"*Saw-ree.*" Wayne looks at the others and jerks a thumb at Robert. "Mr. Poetry Man over here. *Whatevs!*"

"Let's do our best not to be critical," Amaya interjects.

Jerry leans closer and gives Robert a pat on the shoulder. "I know what you mean, Robert. It gets so quiet in my apartment sometimes I don't even know what to do with myself."

"Sometimes I put the television on," Robert says, "but there's never anything I want to see. I don't care for that reality foolishness."

"I don't watch TV," Jerry says, "haven't owned one in years."

"No TV?" Wayne shakes his head in disbelief. "That's crazy, dude."

"Mira and I always preferred board games, listening to our records or curling up with a good book."

"Do you still do those things?" Amaya asks.

"No." He sighs heavily. "These days I go down to the deli instead, get a sandwich and a nice pickle on the side, maybe some soup."

"And do you find that helps?"

"Nothing helps." His eyes fill with tears. "Sorry," he says, clearing his throat.

Amaya retrieves a box of tissues from the floor and offers them to him. "It's perfectly fine for you to feel these emotions right now, so go ahead and give yourself permission to experience them."

Wayne suddenly pipes in. "For Wayne, it's mornings that suck the worst."

Amaya turns to him. "Why are mornings in particular so difficult, Wayne?"

"There's always a couple seconds where I'm all like—maybe it was a dream or some shit—but then I know it's not, and she's still gone and she's never coming back." He shrugs, looking almost bored. "Hate that."

Rain sprays the windows.

Robert begins talking about the walks he and his wife used to take every night after dinner. He relays the story with an expressionless face, recites it in monotone.

"What about you?" Wayne asks once the story is over, but his question is directed at Gordon. "How come you never say anything?"

"Let's remember now," Amaya says, "we've all agreed to respect the rules. One of those rules is that no one has to speak unless they choose to. When and if Gordon wishes to contribute or share, he will. But until then, he has every right to respectfully and quietly listen and observe."

"It's cool," Wayne says, sliding down in his chair like a reprimanded teenager. "I'm just saying everybody else talks and he never does, so sometimes it comes off like all judgmental and shit."

Amaya smiles patiently and gives Gordon a wink. "I'm sure Gordon neither is nor means to be either of those things. Let's move on and talk about—"

"How old are you, son?" Gordon asks Wayne. His hands have finally stopped shaking, he's warming up again and his head is clearer.

It takes Wayne a moment to answer. He seems genuinely surprised Gordon has actually spoken to him. "Thirty-two," he finally says.

"You were two years old when Katy and I were married."

"Okay." Wayne shrugs. "So?"

"So I was married almost as long as you've been alive. I've forgotten more about pain and grief and loss than you'll ever know."

"Let's remember that everyone's experience is valid and their own," Amaya says. "This isn't a competition."

"Yeah, it's not a competition," Wayne tells him. "So don't go getting all pissed at me. I'm just saying—"

"How did your wife die?" Gordon asks.

Wayne looks to the others before answering, as if to be certain he's not the only one hearing the questions. "This an interview or something?"

"You wanted me to talk, didn't you?"

Robert continues to remain quiet, but a slight smile just barely cracks his otherwise stoic expression.

"Well," Amaya says quickly, "maybe Wayne isn't entirely comfortable being questioned like that, Gordon. Maybe you could try—"

"How did she die, Wayne?" Gordon presses.

"A car accident, motherfucker." Wayne sits up then forward in a manner that is almost threatening. Almost, but not quite. "How'd your wife die?"

"All right," Amaya says, "let's all just take it easy. This group is not about being confrontational. Gordon, we all appreciate that you've decided to take part today, but clearly your questions, or the manner in which you're asking them, are upsetting to Wayne. Why don't we talk about that for a moment?

Wayne, without acting out, can you tell us how these questions from Gordon make you feel?"

"They make me *feel* like he's messing with me and disrespecting me when I didn't do anything to him—shit—I don't even know you, man."

"Talk about feeling disrespected. What does that mean to you? How does that make you feel, this notion that you're being disrespected?"

"Makes me feel like I want to break my foot off in his old ass. That's how it makes Wayne feel."

Amaya holds a slender finger up. "Look at me, please, Wayne, not Gordon."

He does.

"We don't threaten here. Not ever. And we don't ridicule here. You know the rules, Wayne, and you seem intent on disregarding them today."

"It's not a threat," Wayne says, sitting back again. "You asked me how it made me feel. I answered you. Never said I'd do it for real."

"Why don't you try?" Gordon stands. "Go ahead. Try."

Wayne laughs. "Sit your bony ass down, Old Man River."

"Gordon," Amaya says, standing as well, "let's calm down, all right?"

Gordon gathers his coat and hat. "I'm sorry for the disruption," he says, turning toward the door. "I shouldn't have come here."

"Gordon, you don't have to leave," Amaya tells him. "These are intense issues we're discussing, and you all have raw nerves exposed, there's bound to be a certain degree of—"

"I think he should answer my question," Wayne says. "You asked me how my old lady died and I told you. How'd yours go?"

Gordon stares at him.

Blood flashes—sprays—spatters—flows like water, rapids crashing over rocks, dragging everything in its path along with it. Drowning… they're all drowning in it…tasting it as it coats their mouths and rushes down their throats, so sticky and sour and metallic…filling their nostrils as they try to breath…their eyes, their ears…their bodies soaked in it, filling with it…drowning…suffocating in blood—

"Why don't you leave him alone, Wayne?" Robert says suddenly.

Wayne turns to him. "Why don't you stay out of it?"

Jerry nervously scratches at the stubble on his chin, his face twisted into a grimace. "This aggression is making me very uncomfortable."

"Me too, Jerry." Amaya laughs lightly in an obvious attempt to cool things down. Very subtly, she positions herself between Gordon and Wayne. "Things are obviously quite heated today—and that's okay, as long as we stay within the rules—but I think we should stop for now. Let's go home and think about the feelings we've had here today. Everyone please be careful, it's nasty out there. Thank you all for coming, and I hope to see you all next week, all right?"

Another burst of rain hits the windows. Gordon looks to them.

Just beyond the blurred and wire-encased panes, stands a dark figure watching them from the street. The figure wears black, loose-fitting clothing and a hood pulled up tight over its head, effectively hiding any detail or features. Gordon can't even be certain if it's a man or woman, though from the size alone, he guesses female.

"And Gordon," Amaya says, gently touching his elbow, "could you stay for a moment, please? I'd like to discuss a few things with you privately."

Her touch causes him to turn away from the window and look at her. She is smiling that usual, infuriatingly warm smile, her eyes bright and beautiful. "Yes," he says softly, "okay."

"He's in trouble now, dog," Wayne laughs and gives Jerry a playful elbow.

Robert shakes his head in disgust, formally shakes everyone's hand good-bye, then turns and walks out. Wayne and Jerry follow behind him, but Wayne makes sure to hold Gordon's gaze as he walks out, a wiseass smirk on his face. When he reaches the door, he gives him a theatrical wave good-bye.

Once the door closes behind them, Gordon looks back to the windows.

The figure is gone. No…not gone…just farther away. There,

barely discernible across the street, standing on the sidewalk. Motionless…watching…

"Is something wrong?" Amaya asks, following his gaze. "You look as if you've seen a ghost."

Slowly, the figure moves away, vanishing into the rain.

"I thought I saw someone watching us," he tells her.

She takes a few steps closer to the windows. "The man across the street in the hooded sweatshirt?"

You saw him too?

"Yes."

"He's moved on now." Amaya closes the blinds on the window, then turns back to Gordon. "There are many lost souls here, Gordon. Some closer than others."

He nods, though he can't be entirely sure what she means. "Dr. Adams, I want to apologize for my behavior, I…"

"There's no need to apologize. Wayne can be rather, well let's just say *difficult* at times." She walks across the room to the counter. "I just wanted to talk with you for a few minutes, privately and without interruption. Would you like a cup of coffee?"

"No. Thank you."

"I hope you won't mind if I have one."

"Not at all."

Amaya pours herself a cup, adds some sugar. "When you first came to group, it was in your paperwork that you'd been to see Dr. Spires previously. I know Carl, he's very good." She stirs her coffee with a plastic spoon. "I hope you don't find this intrusive, but can you tell me why you chose to stop seeing him and decided to try group therapy instead?"

Gordon stands there, trying to think of a response.

"Were you comfortable with Dr. Spires?" she asks.

"I'm not comfortable with anyone."

Amaya gives him a look equal parts compassion and concern. She puts her spoon aside, takes a sip of coffee, then moves closer to him. "And why is that, do you suppose?"

Gordon wants to leave but he's afraid of what's waiting for him out in the rain. "I'm alone a lot," he finally manages. "I have a lot of things on my mind."

"Maybe things you haven't dealt with as yet?" she asks.

When he offers no response, she adds, "Some things you don't know how to deal with or sort out and process effectively on your own?"

"We don't have to do this, I..."

"Would you say you have issues with trust?"

He doesn't answer.

"Do you sometimes feel as if you're all alone, and the rest of the world is out to get you?" She sips more coffee. "Do you ever worry you may be struggling with some issues of paranoia?"

Again, Gordon gives no answer. "Why weren't you able to answer Wayne's question earlier? How did your wife die, Gordon? I know it's not pleasant, but does that question make you uncomfortable?"

"She died in the hospital," he says. "She'd been there for several weeks."

"Why was she in the hospital?"

"Why are you asking me questions you already know the answers to?"

Amaya smiles coyly. "Would you consider returning to Dr. Spires's care?"

Gordon wants to sit down. His knees are sore and his back aches. But he remains standing. "Why?"

"Group therapy isn't for everyone."

"It's all right." Gordon wrestles himself into his raincoat. "I won't be back."

"Please don't misunderstand. I'm not asking you to stop coming."

"It doesn't matter. I'm not coming back."

She frowns. "If you've already made that decision and are committed to it, then I strongly suggest that returning to Dr. Spires is in your best interest."

Gordon holds his hat in his hands, trying to think of something more to say, some way he can get out of there once and for all. He accomplishes neither.

"You didn't *have* to seek professional help," she explains. "But you chose to do so, which means you felt it was necessary on some level. I believe it still is. Do you believe it still is, Gordon?"

He takes a quick look at the windows. The figure has not

returned. There is only the rain. Next he looks to the door. It remains closed. "I don't know."

Amaya takes another sip of coffee, smearing some lipstick on the edge of her cup. "Did something happen today, Gordon?"

How the hell does she know that?

"A man was attacked this morning," he hears himself say, "out in front of my apartment. A homeless man that lives in the park, some punks beat him up."

"You witnessed this?"

Gordon nods.

"How did that make you feel?"

"Frightened. Angry."

"Talk about that."

"I thought we were done for the day."

Amaya slinks past, sits in her chair and crosses her legs. "Do you want to leave, Gordon? Or would you like to stay and talk awhile?"

Although Amaya is half Japanese, sometimes when he looks at her, all Gordon can see are ghosts calling to him from the past. *The eyes*, he thinks, *it's always her eyes, dragging me back to that jungle, that hooch, the fire, the young Vietnamese boy, my gun to his head and everyone screaming. Chaos. Goddamn chaos.* All he sees are that young man's tears. Because that boy knows he is about to die, and no matter what he tells this crazy G.I., nothing is going to change that. He will kill him; execute him right there in his home in front of the rest of his family as his village burns. Maybe because the boy really is Viet Cong and refusing to tell what he knows. Or maybe because he *can* kill him and no one will stop it. Memories of blood spraying from the young man's temple, and the look in his eyes as he falls and dies at Gordon's feet return to the blackest corners of his mind from which they came.

"Are you trying to help me?" he asks.

"Do *you* think I'm trying to help you?"

Standing there awkwardly, his mind begins to race. "I don't know."

"Do you think I'm trying to hurt you, Gordon?"

"I…don't know."

"Why was Katharina in the hospital?"

"You know why." He feels his anger rising, fighting with the fear, the two becoming one. "You've read the paperwork, you know what happened."

"I'd like to hear you say it."

He stumbles, pushes one of the chairs out of the circle with his heel. "Why?"

She puts her coffee down on the floor, then places her hands neatly in her lap. "I'm not trying to torture you, Gordon. I'm here to help you."

"It's all coming back on me now," he says. "Is that what you want to hear?"

"What's coming back on you?"

"The past, the…the memories…"

Amaya stands, but slowly, cautiously. "That's a good thing, Gordon. I know it's painful and frightening, but it's essential in terms of the healing process."

"Healing?" he growls. "There is no healing. Not from what I've done."

Her dark eyes hold his. "What have you done, Gordon?"

What have I done? God in Heaven, what have I done?

"I'm an old man," he says, just above a whisper. "A tired, broken, lonely old man. What would anyone want with me now?"

"My name, *Amaya*, is Japanese," she tells him. "Do you know what it means?"

He shakes his head no.

"Night Rain."

Gordon's hands again begin to tremble. Still clutching his hat, he backs away, out through the opening in the circle of chairs he made previously. "What do you want? I—I made a mistake, it was just thoughts in my head, I—It's not real. None of this is real."

White and black balloons falling…

"It's all right, Gordon. I don't want to hurt you."

Muffled screams echo down a dark corridor…

He continues backing up, closer to the door, shuffling step by step.

Blood…so much blood…

Amaya follows after him, walking slowly. "Do you want to hurt me, Gordon? Is that it? You want to *hurt* me?"

"I never wanted to hurt anyone," he gasps, reaching out with one hand to feel behind him for the door.

"But *did* you hurt someone, Gordon?" Amaya's face and eyes seem darker suddenly, less attractive…less…*human*…

"Please…"

"Do you want to hurt me?" she asks, slowly moving closer still. Her tongue slips free of her mouth and gently traces her pink lips. "Don't be afraid, Gordon. It's going to be all right. Everything's going to be all right if you just let me help you."

His hand finds the door. He pulls it open, stumbles into the dark hallway and moves as quickly as his exhausted body will allow.

When he reaches the front doors to the building, he falls against them, out of breath, and looks back.

There is no one there. But from the shadows comes a terrible whisper…

"Night…Rain."

Gordon pushes through the doors, rushes into the storm, and the open arms of those waiting within it.

FOUR

Though it is not yet night, the storm has left the streets dark and seemingly empty. But somewhere beneath the rain, perhaps within it, there is the sense of life, of motion, of rapid, frenzied movement that may or may not be entirely human. It strikes Gordon as more insect-like, a colony of ants working in furious unison just below the surface, there but hidden in vast tunnels, their bodies and eyes and limbs alien and primal, the antithesis of human. And yet familiarity resides within them, a vague suggestion that they, this *other,* and he, are connected and intertwined. These strange creatures are much closer to human than anyone wants to admit, because if one looks closely enough, long enough, one begins to see oneself in their cold, dark, insect eyes. One begins to feel them within oneself. And one begins to understand.

A foghorn groans in the distance, its sorrowful cry muffled by the downpour. Gordon hurries down the next alleyway he comes to. *Need to get off the main streets, it's not safe, they—they're watching me. I can feel them watching me.* At the end of the alley stands a rotting chain link fence too high for him to climb. Luckily there is a hole torn in one section.

Someone before him cut an opening in the fence, then bent it back enough for most people to squeeze through.

Pulling his raincoat in tight around him, Gordon forces himself into the opening and through to the other side. Another stretch of alley awaits him. Rain rushes from the gutters, flooding the pavement. The water is nearly to his ankles.

He leans against the brick wall of one building, pulls the brim of his hat down, tucks chin to chest and tries to catch his breath. Something tells him to look up. Something instinctual. Gordon obeys. His eyes drift upward, through the rain, and focus on a second-story window filled with pale light. A female figure undresses in the window; her silhouette segmented into pieces, cast through an open venetian blind. A trick of the backlight, it looks as if someone has sliced her body into a series of identically spaced portions that somehow still move as one.

The rain spatters against his face and eyes. He closes them and paws them dry. But in the darkness, he sees. *People in formal dress celebrating and laughing as champagne flows…and there, across the room…a vision…*

Gordon watches the shadow-woman undress, but it is not her he sees. It is only Katy. Always Katy. His sweet, wonderful Katy, the only woman he has ever wanted. The only woman he has ever loved.

All the years they shared fill his mind, rush past like a sped-up film.

The most beautiful woman he has ever seen…watching…watching him… before looking away with a coy smile… those gorgeous eyes, so full of love and understanding…seeing only him…

So many wonderfully happy years spent together—so much love, such joy—and all of it gone like a wisp of smoke. No. Not gone. Stolen.

"I'm sure it's nothing serious."

The woman moves away from the window, and after a moment, the light goes out. "You lied to me," Gordon mumbles. "You lied to me."

"Of course…"

He moves on, comes out onto a busier, well-lit street. The city is alive here, louder, bustling and vibrant. Cars rush past. People populate the area, hurrying in the rain. Umbrellas everywhere. He sees an available cab out in front of a diner halfway down the block. Harry insisted on paying the tab at the bar earlier, so Gordon still has eighteen dollars in his wallet, but doesn't want to blow it on a cab. He squints through the rain, scanning the area until he locates a subway entrance diagonally across the street.

He crosses the street, ignoring the blare of car horns, and then hobbles down the stairs and into the subway station. Free of the rain, he removes his hat, shakes it out, then replaces it as he moves along the tunnel toward a bank of turnstiles. He is not alone here, but it is not as busy as it is on the street, which he finds odd.

Everyone seems suspect now.

Perhaps they always have.

Despite the weakness and aching in his legs and back, Gordon keeps moving, head down and avoiding eye contact whenever possible, while still keeping a lookout for those stalking him. *I know you're there*, he thinks. *And you know I know.*

Moments later he finds himself waiting on the platform with a few others. His train arrives quickly. He boards and gratefully collapses onto an open bench as the doors slide closed and the train lurches forward. They slink off into the dark tunnel, the interior lights blinking once, then twice, as the train picks up speed.

There are only four other people in the car. A tall, middle-aged Sikh with bloodshot eyes stands near the doors, even though there are plenty of places to sit. A young man in a wrinkled business suit, raincoat and scuffed wingtips sits slumped on the bench to Gordon's left, a leather briefcase across his lap. Clearly inebriated and either asleep or passed out, he sways with the motion of the train, eyes closed and mouth ajar. A couple in their late teens sits directly across from him. Both eel thin, they are dressed entirely in black, share an apparent fondness for black eyeliner, black lipstick and black hair dye, and sport a wide array of piercings and tattoos. Holding hands, they sit quietly together in a posture both sweet and formal.

Gordon wonders what they all see when they look at him.

An old man on his last legs, he thinks, *a wasted shell of what was once a useful and vibrant human being, a wrinkled old bag of bones waiting to die.*

He has a chill he just can't seem to shake, but bundles up in his raincoat as best he can anyway. It does no good. Maybe Hell isn't a lake of fire at all, but an endless world of ice and snow, a freezing block of ice. Or perhaps Gordon knows better. Perhaps he knows all too well exactly what Hell is. Because the question is not *does* Hell exist, but *where* and *how* does it exist?

And if there is a Hell…

The drunken businessman groans in his sleep and slumps a bit farther down in his seat. His briefcase teeters precariously at the edges of his knees but somehow remains where it is.

No one but Gordon seems to notice.

The train barrels around a bend in the tunnel, and the lights blink once more.

Moments later, the train makes its first stop, and the Sikh gets off. The goth couple rises to leave as well. "Hey, mister," the girl says in a squeaky little voice that in no way suits her, "you okay? Do you need help or something?"

Gordon looks up at her questioningly. He wants to answer, to thank her for caring, and to let her know he's not okay. But the words catch in his throat and slowly die there.

The couple stares at him with their black eyes. "C'mon," the boy finally says, dragging his girlfriend along with him by the hand. "We'll miss our stop."

Gordon watches them leave, then turns and looks out the window so he can still see them as the train pulls out. The couple stands on the platform, the boy obviously annoyed but the girl still concerned.

Gordon's eyes remain locked on hers until the train pulls out, leaving the couple behind as it disappears into darkness.

I must look awful, he thinks, *like death…like death…*

He turns around, sits back, and realizes someone else has taken the couple's place on the bench across from him. A woman in a long coat, a red dress and black high-heels sits before him, her head bowed so that her face is hidden behind thick auburn hair. Gordon cannot be sure of her age, but on cue, the woman raises her head just enough to reveal that she is much younger than he is, and has likely not yet seen her thirty-fifth birthday.

But there is something else. He knows this woman.

No, I…it's not possible…

The woman bows her head again, and her face disappears from view.

You're mistaken. It can't be, it—it's not her. It's not possible.

No one but this woman boarded at the last stop, so Gordon is now alone with her and the passed-out businessman. He does his best to sit very still, and tries to control the tremors of fear throttling him from head to toe.

It looks like her, that's all. It looks like her, resembles her, but it's not her because it can't be. It's just your tired, failing old senile mind playing its nasty tricks on you again, making you think you're seeing and hearing things that aren't there.

But Gordon knows better. He knows full well what is and isn't there.

She's dead. You know she's dead.

The train sways as something on the floor catches Gordon's eye. A dark crimson puddle is slowing spreading out from beneath the woman's shoes, creeping across the floor between them, growing as it moves toward him.

"You're bleeding," he hears himself say, his voice raspy and shaking. "You there, you—ma'am—you're *bleeding.*"

The woman slowly raises her head. Blue eyes peer out through the hair hanging in her face. She is void of expression, and her eyes are glassy and lifeless, like the soulless gaze of a doll.

Gordon slams shut his eyes, squeezing them tight before slowly reopening them in the hopes that the woman will be gone. She is not.

It can't be—he knows this, understands it—and yet there she is, still sitting right there in front of him. He is not mistaken. He is not asleep. He is not drunk or stoned. "Am I crazy?" he says aloud. "Or am I damned?"

"Maybe you're both," the woman replies in a deadpan voice that gurgles as if she's drowning in his own bodily fluids.

Gordon struggles to his feet, reaches for a handgrip hanging above and manages to catch one before falling. He holds on with all his might, but his muscles are not what they used to be, and a burning sensation fires up through his shoulder and down his back between his shoulder blades. The blood on the floor is closer now, so close that he has to shuffle to his left to avoid stepping in it.

The woman reaches inside her low-cut dress with a pale

hand, clearly searching for something. But as her hand goes deeper between her ample breasts, the sickening sound of unseen things tearing and breaking follows, and then comes the sound of something wet being wrenched free. The horrible sounds echo through the car.

No, I—I have to get out of here, I—

Gordon whirls round, still clutching the handgrip, and sees the door at the far end of the car. He has to make it there, has to get away from this now or he'll never leave this train. He knows this. He will die here.

"Lamb of God," the woman says in her gurgling voice. "You take away the sins of the world, have mercy on us."

Gordon heads for the door but stumbles and falls against the wall of the train. He twists and pushes himself back to his feet, just as the woman removes her hand from her cleavage to reveal what she's gone looking for. Her heart, dripping and coated in shiny crimson, there, in the palm of her bloody hand…

"Lamb of God, you take away the sins of the world, grant us *peace.*"

Mind shattering, Gordon staggers toward the door. When he reaches it, a strange and sudden calm washes over him. The fear remains, but his body and mind are no longer fighting it.

He watches her awhile, lying there next to him. She isn't asleep but her eyes are closed as if she is. He reaches out, tenderly strokes her cheek, then brings his fingers up and runs them across her forehead. She is warm and soft and beautiful. And he is happy. For the first time in his life, he is happy. Not only because he's loved, but also because he *loves. He loves her so much he sometimes doesn't know what to do with himself or his emotions. Sometimes it literally feels as if he might burst apart with joy. Of course their life together isn't perfect, but my God, it's good. And it's as close as he can ever hope to come. He has never known anyone like her.*

Her eyes open and she blinks a few times, bringing him into focus.

"What is it?" she asks dreamily.

"Nothing," he tells her, stroking her forehead. "It's just…I love you."

She smiles, and it is the most beautiful and wondrous thing he has ever seen.

"I love you too, Gordon."

"Sometimes I wonder why."

Katy arches an eyebrow as she slinks an arm around his waist. "Why would you wonder about such things?"

"I can't imagine what you see in me."

"Well, what do you see in me?"

"You're smart and beautiful and loving," he says. "You're patient, and kind."

"You're all of those things too."

He laughs lightly. "No."

"To me you are."

"Maybe to you, but—"

"Isn't that all that matters?"

She winks playfully.

He kisses her cheek. "Maybe it is."

"You worry too much about the past."

"You know I don't like to talk about—"

"I understand." She places her finger to his lips. "But you have to let it go. You have to forgive yourself and let yourself be happy. You have to let yourself be loved. We found each other. We found happiness with each other. Who knows how long any of us have in this life? Embrace it, enjoy every moment while we can."

"Do you remember the night we met?"

"Of course, don't be silly."

"The New Year's Eve ball. You were the most beautiful woman I'd ever seen."

"Stop," she chuckles.

"It's true."

"I'm not the most beautiful woman anyone's ever seen."

"You are to me." This time he winks.

"Touché."

"You didn't like me much that night, but I loved you the moment I saw you."

"I didn't know you."

"You weren't interested."

"I gave you my phone number, didn't I?"

"After I badgered you and followed you around like a lost puppy for two hours."

A mischievous smile purses her lips. "Maybe I felt a bit sorry for you."

"But not sorry enough to go out with me. The first two times I called and asked you out you gave me excuses and said no."

"But eventually I said yes."

"What was it that finally changed your mind?"

"Third time's the charm?"

"No, Katy, seriously."

"Maybe you wore me down. Then once I got to know you and saw how sweet you were, how could I not fall in love with you too?"

"You saved my life," he says, the words catching in his throat.

"And you mine."

He shakes his head no. "You saved me, Katy. I was nothing before you."

"Gordon…"

"Nothing. Nothing until I met you."

She pulls him closer, wrapping both arms around him. "Shhh."

"I love you so much."

"What's gotten in to you tonight?" she asks, her breath hot on his neck. "You never talk like this."

"I'm sorry. I should tell you how much I love you every day."

"I know how much you love me, sweetheart."

"Do you?" he asks. "Do you really?"

"Can anyone ever truly know how much someone else loves them?"

No, he thinks, they can't. And sometimes, they shouldn't.

"I'm sorry," he says, holding her close.

"Whatever for?"

"Everything."

The train screeches, shattering Gordon's memories. Still

slumped against the door, he looks back. The businessman is out cold, but there is no one else in the car.

With a hearty tug, he pulls open the door, slips into the next car and slams the door closed behind him.

The train races on, hurtling through the dark tunnels beneath the city.

FIVE

Southeast Asia. Exhausted, battered and bloody, he clings to the trunk of a twisted and fallen tree, floats along the filthy river... drifting...toward what he doesn't know. But he is in Hell. That much he knows. And he will not be leaving anytime soon. There is a good chance he will never leave, though he no longer much cares. It's been a very long time since he's given a damn one way or another. If he dies, so be it. If nothing else, it will end this horror, and whatever may or may not await him on the other side cannot be any worse. Of this he is certain, even as he clings to this dead floating thing, watching the jungle on either side drift past like a dream. So much black smoke rising and twisting from burning things and burning people, if only he could sleep for just a little while it would all go away. But if he does, he will slip from his tree and sink down into the filthy brown and bloody water, and he will never come back. Would it be so bad? Why doesn't he just do it then and get it over with? Because he will not give Hell the satisfaction, and will not go willingly. If it wants him, it will have to take him, rip him away and carry him off to oblivion kicking and screaming.

All around him, savaged bodies—some of them just pieces—bob about like demonic buoys. He used to see the dead in his nightmares, but they no longer afford him that, they come all the time now, as relentlessly as they did in life. But they belong to the river now. It has taken them just as it tries to take him, pulling at him, hoping to drag him deep beneath the surface. Everything smells of gasoline, fecal matter and urine, of charred and burning human flesh. Death.

In the distance, he sees an assault boat headed toward him. A

Rolling Stones tune blares from its speakers. Once again, he will survive and cheat death while others are slaughtered all around him. They will pluck him from this river of evil, but not before it baptizes him in its sins…and his own…leaving a part of him in this river forever. A part he can never regain. Like so many others, he is ghosted in this jungle, just another pale spirit far from home, watching from the muddy banks of the river, coated in its blood and cloaked in its lies.

As Gordon walks along the sidewalk, his nightmares leave him, and he sees the cemetery in the distance, at the top of a hill. The rain has lessened but still falls in a heavy swirling mist. He pushes himself up the hill, stopping twice to catch his breath before reaching the gates. They stand open. He looks around. Here, at the outskirts of the city, there are far fewer buildings, less concrete, more trees and grass, fewer cars and fewer people. It is not as easy to hide here, and though he appears to be alone, he knows he's not.

He moves through the gates, his shoes squishing the muddy grass along the path to the first section of burial plots. An ocean of graves awaits him—crypts, tombs, headstones, mausoleums and angelic statues—stretching for far as the eye can see. And yet, ironically, Gordon feels nothing of the dead here, with its great corridors of meaningless stone and rotting flesh, its monuments to dust.

It's been a long while since Gordon has been here, so it takes him a moment to remember, but he eventually does, and he finds himself walking along the narrow paved paths between the graves. In time, he arrives at the one he has come to visit, a small headstone of dark gray granite. A cross is etched into the front, and beneath it is Katharina's name, date of birth and date of death. Alongside hers is Gordon's name and date of birth, followed by a dash, and then nothing. How strange it is to see one's name already carved into a gravestone, awaiting one's inevitable arrival. A cracked green plastic planter lies on its side in front of the stone, the bright flowers it had once been filled with long dead. Gordon remembers coming here the last time with Harry in tow, months ago now, and how they'd brought the planter. He does his best to ignore thoughts and visions of her body under his feet and encased in that horrible coffin. His eyes return to her name, and it quickly blurs through his tears. "Katy," he whispers. "My Katy."

"Gordon..."

The wind rustles the branches of a nearby tree, drawing his attention to it. He rubs his eyes until they clear, and then he looks again. But he was not mistaken. There *is* something in the tree... something that doesn't belong, sitting there on a thick branch not too far from the ground. He takes a few steps toward the tree, which is still about thirty feet away, then squints through the misting rain.

What the hell is that?

Gordon takes another step, and then he sees. A man dressed in black sits on the branch, watching him with a wry smile, his legs dangling and swinging to and fro the way a child's might. He knows what he's seeing, but his mind can't quite grasp it.

"Hello, Gordon," the man says. His voice is smooth and deep, almost musical, and he appears to be somewhere in his thirties. He is so good-looking he's nearly pretty, with striking ice-blue eyes and thick dark hair that hangs to his shoulders combed straight back. His goatee is perfectly trimmed and accentuates his bright, perfectly white teeth. "I knew you'd come. I've been waiting."

"How do you know my name?"

"I know everyone's name." He slowly slides from the branch and drops to the ground, effortlessly landing on his feet. His long black leather coat flutters in the wind as he strolls closer. "But some better than others," he adds, the same wry smile on his handsome face. "We've met before. Don't tell me you can't remember."

He *does* seem familiar, in a faraway sense, like a distant memory at the very edge of a long-ago dream. But he doesn't want him to be familiar at all. He doesn't want to know or be anywhere near this man. "I've lost my mind," Gordon says. "That's it, isn't it? I've lost my mind."

The man arches an eyebrow. "What makes you think it's yours to lose?" He delicately scratches at his chin with slightly long, tapered, manicured fingernails. There are rings on every finger of both hands. Silver, ornate rings that look like snakes and demons. He combs his hair back, hooking it behind his ears, and reveals silver dagger earrings dangling from each lobe. "Did you really think you'd find what you were looking for here? They're all gone from this place, Gordon. There's nothing here but bones."

Disjointed flashes of horror blink across his mind's eye like lightning, and he suddenly feels sick to his stomach. "Who are you?"

"Who do you think I am?"

"You're not real."

The man grins and widens his brilliant blue eyes. "Neither are you."

"What do you want?"

The man's smile slowly fades but he offers no response.

"Leave me alone." Gordon moves back. "I'm just an old man."

The man motions to Katharina's grave with a slow sweep of his hand. "But we have things to discuss, you and I."

"I don't know you, we—I've never seen you before in my life. You're lying."

"I'm the King of Lies, old friend." The man's smile returns. "But remember this. The damned burn not in hellfire, but the light of truth."

"It was just thoughts in my head," Gordon mutters, a hand to his mouth as if this might somehow prevent him from saying anything more.

"I'm the Rain Man, Gordon." He looks to the sky. The rain picks up, changes from a mist to a steady drizzle. Not far away, thunder rumbles and rolls across the heavens. "Kneel before me."

Again, Gordon backs away, and this time he loses his balance, slips and nearly falls. "Stay away!"

"You think some rotting bloodless mannequin in a box can save you?"

"Katy was everything, I—she was all I had!"

"No, Gordon, you had me too. You've always had me too." The man opens his arms and spreads them wide like great black wings, his leather coat billowing in the wind. "And now I have you."

Gordon hobbles to Katy's grave and drops to his knees. "Help me," he gasps. "Help me, Katy. Tell me what to do, I—please—tell me what to do." Behind him, Gordon hears the man coming closer, his boots squishing the wet earth with each step. No longer able to remain upright, Gordon slumps forward into the wet grass and mud, his muffled pleas deadened by the din of a suddenly pouring rain…

Night, in the city…

Gordon walks the streets for hours, as he often does when he's troubled or needs to think or sort something out. On this night, after a couple hours wandering the city, he comes upon a small basement nightclub nestled between several quirky storefronts in an otherwise quiet neighborhood in the West Village. It is the small funky sign that first catches his attention. It reads: NIGHT-RAIN CLUB. He is tired from walking and needs a drink. Several drinks, actually, and this seems like a quiet little place where no one will bother him and he can drown his sorrows in peace.

He descends the steps, slips through a black door painted to resemble a starry night sky, and finds himself in a small club. The modest space consists of a bar against one wall, tables and chairs scattered throughout, and a tiny high-gloss dance floor. A jazz trio plays a mellow tune from a corner stage, and everything is washed in a seductive blue hue from the neon track lighting that runs along the ceiling and walls and even outlines the front of the heavily backlit bar. Several tables are occupied but only one of the ten stools at the bar is in use. Gordon considers escaping to an empty table in the rear of the club, but at the last minute decides to sit at the bar instead.

He can think of nothing but the woman he met at the New Year's Eve ball.

Katharina. Katy to her friends, she told him.

He has been infatuated with her since he laid eyes on her weeks ago, and has been pursuing her ever since. But so far, nothing, she seems to have no interest in him whatsoever. Perhaps as friends, but Gordon wants more, needs more.

"I'm in love with her," he told his friend Harry.

"You're obsessed, mate. You can't be in love, you barely know her."

"I know enough. I know I fell in love with her the moment I saw her."

He feels silly even thinking such things. It's not like him, not his way, yet he cannot help himself. He's been waiting all his life for this woman, he just didn't know it…until he saw her…and then the realization hit him like an anvil.

"Evening, welcome to the Night-Rain Club." The bartender, a stocky, spike-haired man in a gold vest, black pants and a white shirt, greets him with something close to a smile.

Gordon orders a scotch and soda on the rocks and does his best to relax and enjoy the music. But he has too much on his mind. Harry's right, he thinks, he is obsessed. But there are worse things, aren't there? For so long he has lived under a veil of darkness, of past horrors and a lonely life he has been unable to let anyone be a part of in any real way. And now, for the first time, he sees a chance—a real chance—to find happiness. If only he could convince her to spend some time with him, then she'd see…

The bartender delivers his drink, then moves away.

Gordon drinks awhile, listens to a set of particularly hypnotic jazz tunes as they drift soulfully through the small space. He closes his eyes, pictures Katy…

"Is it a woman?" The sultry voice to Gordon's left startles him. He turns to see that a beautiful woman in her mid-thirties has slid onto the stool next to his despite the fact that all the other spots at the bar remain vacant. "I'm sorry?" he asks.

"You look troubled," the woman says, smiling ever so slightly. "Is it a woman?"

Gordon forces a grin. "Is it that obvious?"

She shrugs playfully. "Isn't it always a woman?"

"You may have a point."

"Lucinda," she says, extending a delicate hand with nails painted fire-red.

He shakes her hand. It is warm and soft. "Gordon."

"Very nice to meet you, Gordon." She brushes a strand of auburn

hair from her beautiful blue eyes and smiles, this time revealing bright white teeth.

"Pleasure."

She signals the bartender. "You don't mind if I sit so close, do you? I was hoping for some conversation tonight."

"I'm not usually one for a lot of conversation, but be my guest."

The bartender arrives and gives Lucinda a knowing wink. "Looking gorgeous as ever this evening, Lucy."

"Careful, flattery might get you everything you ever wanted."

"If only," he chuckles. "The usual?"

"Let's make it a Bloody Mary tonight,

Bernie," she says, and once he's gone, returns her attention to Gordon. "So do tell, Gordon, why so gloomy?"

"Nothing all that interesting, I'm afraid."

"Let me guess." Lucinda looks into his eyes. "Love?"

Gordon raises his glass to her. "You're good."

"Hardly." She laughs lightly, but it is a deep and bawdy laugh that doesn't quite fit her otherwise delicate appearance. In a long, dangerously low-cut ruby red dress and black spike heels, she has a face and body that would turn any man's head, and more than a few women's. Her makeup is a bit heavy, especially her bold red lipstick and dark eye shadow, but she manages it without appearing cheap. Still, she practically drips sex, and carries herself like someone who knows what she's got and how it affects other people, especially straight men, and is in no way shy about utilizing it. In fact, if anything, it appears to amuse her.

Gordon can't decide if this is because she considers herself superior, or if she simply doesn't take herself all that seriously. He decides it's the latter, but he can't be entirely certain. Although talking about his troubles with this stranger is just about the last thing he wants to do, there is something so charming about her, so disarming, he already knows he will do just that, because she also seems harmless and genuine.

"Troubles at home with the wife?" she asks.

He holds his left hand up to show her the lack of a wedding ring. "Not married."

"Girlfriend then?"

"No. Not yet anyway."

"Ah-hah. Hoping for love but not yet sure she feels the same?"

"At this point, I'm just hoping she'll give me a chance."

"And if she does?"

"That she'll see we were meant to be."

"Mmm, fate." She widens her eyes, his answer having noticeably aroused her. She leans closer, her ample breasts crushed against him as she whispers in his ear. "Are you a believer in such things?"

The bartender delivers Lucinda's drink. Gordon doesn't answer until he's gone and she sits back. "I'm not sure what I believe. I just want a chance."

She raises her glass. "To chances."

He lifts his glass and gently taps it against hers.

"And to taking full advantage of them when they're offered," she adds.

As they drink, Lucinda's free hand drops beneath the bar, slides onto his knee and gives it a gentle squeeze. Gordon does not remove it.

Neither does she.

A church bell rings, breaking through the sound of the rain. Gordon pushes himself up. Still on his knees, he sways but catches himself on Katy's stone. His face is wet and smeared with mud, his hat crushed down in front. He digs in his pocket for a handkerchief, finds it and wipes himself clean. For several moments he remains where he is, partly because he is afraid to look behind him, and partly because he isn't sure if he yet has the strength to get himself back to his feet. But he knows he can't stay out here forever. He's soaked to the bone and freezing, a potentially lethal combination for someone his age.

Finally, he looks behind him. The man is not there. He looks to the tree, where he'd first seen him. Nothing. Yet the fear, the terror, remains.

Memories of long-lost nights cling to him, forcing him to remember things he has tried for years to forget, to convince himself are not true and never took place.

I'm the King of Lies, old friend.

Using the headstone for purchase, Gordon pushes himself up and onto his feet. The front of his raincoat is wet and stained with dirt and mud, but he doesn't bother to clean it off, because things are moving inside him, slithering about, coming awake and creeping out from the darkest and most diseased corners of his mind. And he cannot escape them. Not anymore. Not ever again.

"Katy," he says, stroking the stone. "I never meant for you to be a part of any of this. The darkness was mine, not yours. You were the light, always the light. I had no right, I—please—forgive me."

The damned burn not in hellfire, but the light of truth…

The church bell ringing in the distance changes to bellowing laughter, hideous and evil, rolling across the sea of graves through the steady rain like the nightmare it is.

Night is falling.

Gordon begins to run, slowly and painfully—awkwardly—but as best as his old bones will allow.

And the Devil, he sleeps, his demonic dreams growing stronger and crawling free to roam the streets, thieves beneath liquid skies, where the lost, the broken and the forgotten wander in darkness—their eyes put out—seeking redemption they will never find, and deliverance they will never know.

SIX

The worst memories come at night.

Gordon locks his apartment up tight, pulls the shades on the windows and uses only a small lamp in the den for illumination. Otherwise, the apartment is cloaked in darkness. Although he took a hot shower and changed into fresh dry clothes, and has even wrapped a heavy blanket around him, he cannot seem to get warm, and the aches and pains in his joints and in his back refuse to lessen.

For more than an hour, he sits in his chair with an old shoebox on his lap filled with old photographs, notes, cards and knickknacks he and Katy shared over their years together. These things—many of them hers—are items he hasn't looked at or touched for a very long time. But now he cannot stop. He rifles through them, his arthritic fingers fighting him at every turn. Each birthday, anniversary or Christmas card, each photograph or item has a story, a meaning, and a memory.

And for the first time in years,

Gordon remembers them all.

If he listens very carefully, and everything is very quiet—the traffic and city sounds outside his windows muted—he swears he can hear the most beautiful and frightening singing he has ever heard. It's so very far away, but he can hear it. Male and female voices sing together in mesmerizing harmony. They sound like angels—or how he imagines angels might sound—their haunting voices building and building in song to a heartbreaking crescendo that makes him want to collapse to his knees and weep.

But he does neither.

With shaking hands, he continues to sift through the photographs until he can no longer take it. He replaces the lid and puts the shoebox aside, but remains in his chair, exhausted.

Rain spatters the windows. He can no longer see it, but he can hear it out there trying to get in, trying to get at him, to soak him down. Not to cleanse, but to scald, a baptism in acid.

The voices of angels soften then die amidst the mounting storm sounds.

Gordon reaches for his pipe, which he has prepared earlier, and lights it, drawing the pungent smoke deep into his already wheezing lungs and holding it there long as he can. He coughs out a cloud, then hits the pipe again, getting mostly a resin hit the second time. Within seconds of exhaling he can feel the pot taking effect, dancing through his system and causing his temples to tingle. But still, he cannot relax.

He puts the pipe aside, struggles out of the chair and walks through the dark apartment, down a short hallway to his bedroom. He stands in front of his bureau for some time, just staring at it, willing himself to reach out and pull open the bottom drawer.

He has not opened that drawer in months. Tonight, he decides, he will. If it takes him all night, he will open that drawer.

Without turning on a light, he crouches low enough to reach the knobs on the bottom drawer, grips them tight as he can and pulls the drawer open.

Clothes. Mostly T-shirts and sweatshirts, a couple lightweight sweaters and a hoodie he's never worn. Some items are wrinkled and stuffed in there haphazardly, while others are folded nicely and look like new.

Don't think about it. Just do it. Do it, you pathetic old fuck. Do it.

Gordon grabs the top layer of clothes, pulls them free of the drawer and tosses them aside to the floor. It is enough to reveal the heavy, clear plastic bag that lies beneath them.

He slams shut his eyes, but the visions refuse to let go. Nothing can stop them now. Perhaps it's better this way. It's time.

Slowly, he reaches through the shadows and touches the

bag. Nausea rises, bubbles at the base of his throat, and he nearly vomits. But the pot has leveled him out enough to keep him from losing it completely, and with a few deep breaths and a little concentration, Gordon manages to pull the bag free, feeling its weight and all that it means as he straightens up and heads back out into the den.

Once he has returned to the sparse light, he holds the bag out before him, studying the faded white tag with the handwriting on it, and the large blue letters written across it that read: evidence—do not tamper.

"I'm sure it's nothing serious."

The light shows him now, brings him back.

A shattered mirror over a sink, sprayed with blood and body fluids, pieces of brain and skull…

A gun. *The* gun.

I can't make it, Gordon…I can't make it…

He remembers the policeman who initially confiscated it, as evidence at the scene, was the same one who returned it to him when the investigation had ended.

"It's your property and a legally licensed firearm," he'd told Gordon, standing there in the doorway and holding the bag out for him. "By law we have to return it to you once the investigation is complete and it is no longer required as evidence."

"I don't…I don't want this," he'd stammered.

"No, sir," the cop said, "I imagine not. But as I say, the law states that we return it to you, it's your property."

"Christ," he said, the revolver visible through the clear plastic, "it still—can't you see it still has blood on it?"

"We return it directly from evidence, sir. I'm sorry."

Gordon has never taken it out of the plastic bag. Now, he does.

He grips the revolver, pulls it free of the bag and holds it up in front of his face, studying it as if he's never before seen such a thing. There is still blood along the end of the barrel and on the grip. Though long-dried, he touches it with his finger anyway. It is crusty and rough, but it is all he has.

Before the emotion becomes too great, he tosses the bag

aside and goes to the kitchen. He finds a box of ammunition in a drawer next to the refrigerator, and dumps some rounds out on the counter. He loads the revolver with six bullets, then takes it and those that remain in the box and stuff them into the pocket of his raincoat, which he has left hanging on a coatrack just inside the front door.

He ignores the blinking light on his old answering machine, which is telling him he has four messages. Harry, no doubt, checking up on him, making sure he's all right. *Well, no, Harry, I'm not all right. I'm not all right at all.* His old friend means well, and Gordon knows this, but he also knows that he's headed somewhere he can only go alone.

Gordon scoops up the shoebox, feeling empty inside now, and carries it over to the kitchen. He places it in the sink, then gets a small can of lighter fluid, a book of matches and a roll of duct tape from a nearby drawer. He places the tape on the counter, soaks the box down with lighter fluid, and then stands there awhile, staring at the old shoebox and everything it means.

"I can't make it, Gordon…I can't make it…"

He strikes the match and it flares to life.

"Neither can I, love," he says softly.

Wind sprays rain against the windows as the storm furiously lashes the apartment building, fighting to claw its way in. But it's too late. Gordon drops the match, watches as it twists and tumbles and falls through the air—he'd swear in slow motion—until it lands atop the shoebox.

A burst of flame ignites and rises from the sink in a single feverish wave.

Gordon watches it, mesmerized by the dancing flames and the smoke billowing about. Slowly, he clenches his fist and brings it closer to the fire.

Oddly, his hands have finally stopped shaking.

Tightening his fist, he pushes it into the flames, gritting his teeth as it burns his hand and wrist. The pain is nearly unbearable. Nearly. He holds his hand still as possible, allowing the fire to do its best. He can smell his flesh burning, and the pain becomes agonizing. Still, he does not move his hand. His entire body quakes, but he holds it in the fire, watching it burn and feeling every moment of it.

It reminds him of death, of the jungles. It reminds him of killing, of how it feels to kill. How it feels to die as you kill, and how one cannot ever be free of the other.

Yanking his fist back from the fire, he lunges forward, and with his other hand, turns on the faucet. The box sizzles and is quickly extinguished, as a small cloud of black smoke rolls from the sink across the kitchen and into the den.

Gordon grabs a hand towel from the counter, soaks it under the tap, then wraps his damaged hand with it. With his teeth, he starts the duct tape. Using his good hand, he begins wrapping it around the towel to hold it in place. He wraps it again and again, making it tight as he can stand. It makes the pain even worse, but he continues until it looks like some sort of mitt or cast; then he lumbers into the other room to open a window before the smoke detectors go off.

The pain is blinding now, turning to a different kind of agony, a searing and rolling pain that pulses from the burned area up into his elbow and upper arm. It is so horrific he's sure he'll lose consciousness. But he doesn't.

He goes to the double windows facing the street, releases the shade on one and forces the window open. Slumping against the sill, his vision blurs as rain invades his apartment, spraying him in the face and across his neck. Despite the cold, he is sweating profusely, and his heart races with such ferocity he can only hope he's well on his way to a heart attack or a stroke.

But then voices down on the street draw his attention.

Three of the teenagers that assaulted the homeless man earlier are standing beneath the awning of the convenience store on the corner, laughing and smoking cigarettes. They talk loudly to each other in an attempt to be heard over the wind and rain.

The phone begins to ring. He ignores it, closes the window and pulls on his raincoat and hat. He looks back at the phone, then decides to answer it after all. He already knows who it is.

"Hello."

"Gordo, Christ on the cross, I've been trying to get hold of you all day."

"What do you want, Harry?"

"What do I want?"

"Yes. What do you want?"

"Are you all right?"

Momentarily distracted by the pain, Gordon doesn't answer.

"Gordo? Are you there?"

"I'm here."

"Are you all right?"

"No."

"Talk to me."

"I have to go, Harry."

"Go? Where? It's after dark and storming out there. Are you stoned again, you damn fool?"

"Everything's all mixed up, Harry. It's all running together and I…I can't remember them separately, one without the other, I…I've lost track of where one memory ends and another begins."

"Okay, look you—you stay there and you put some coffee on, you hear me? I'll get a cab and I'll be there in—"

"I won't be here, Harry."

"I'm leaving now."

"I'm sorry," Gordon says.

"Don't be sorry, just stay put."

"Good-bye."

"You ornery, stubborn sonofabitch, will you just listen a minute?"

"Good-bye, Harry. Thank you for being my friend." He clears his throat awkwardly. "I know I wasn't always the best friend to you, but—"

"Nonsense. You're my best friend, always have been."

"I can't run anymore, Harry."

"It's okay," Harry insists. "We'll sit and talk, have some coffee—hell a few drinks if you want—and we'll decide what to do, all right? Just let me help you, Gordo. It'll be all right if you just let me help you."

He has heard these exact words before. Even as Gordon hangs up, he can hear Harry yelling for him to stay where he is.

Gordon returns to the window, sees that the boys are still out there.

They will finish what the pain has begun. They will set him free.

This night, and all of its demons, will set him free.

SEVEN

In the movie running through his head, Gordon's body is young and powerful. He jogs along the deserted beach, giving Katy a piggyback. It is late and the moon is bright and full in the clear night sky. Having split a bottle of wine earlier at their bungalow, they ventured out to the sands to be silly and romantic as young couples are often wont to do.

Gordon runs until he can run no more, finally sinking down onto his knees in the wet sand along the water's edge. As he topples over onto his side, he gently dumps Katy into drier nearby sand. They don't realize it then, so early in their marriage, but this will be the only major vacation they will ever take. His line job at the furniture factory, and hers as a receptionist at a dentist's office, will not allow for extravagant trips to the Bahamas. But they will remember this trip and cherish it forever. It is a time before the bills become so great, a time before they have any worries to speak of, a time when they are both young and healthy and wildly in love with each other. Alive. They are alive. And they will never be this alive again.

Gordon rolls closer to her, and kisses her. "One day," he tells her, "we're going to grow old together, and I'm going to bring you back here, to this island, on this beach, and we're going to do this all over again."

"I hope so, love," she whispers.

He cups her face in his hands, but she slowly begins to disintegrate, crumbling to pieces right before his eyes. Running through his fingers, so many handfuls of sand he can no longer grasp, a castle he can never rebuild, she is gone and he is alone, the water lapping at his feet as it rolls in off the ocean…

The sand turns to rain, and as Gordon steps out onto the

street and into the storm, he sees the teenagers still huddled under the corner convenience store's awning. Hands in his raincoat pockets, he fades back into the shadows next to his building, and watches the street awhile.

"Yo, G., what you doin' out here in the rain?"

Gordon turns to his right. The young man he buys his marijuana from is standing at the mouth of an alley a few feet away. Dressed in a New York Knicks jacket and jeans low on his hips, a baseball cap turned sideways on his head, he protects himself from the rain best he can in a doorway just inside the alley.

"You need some smoke?"

"No," Gordon tells him.

"Then where you goin'? Ain't safe after dark, you know dat."

Gordon looks back at the kids on the corner.

"You don't want nothin' to do with them neither," his dealer says. "You stay away from them, you hear? Them fools beat that poor old homeless motherfucker into the hospital today. Was gone by the time Five showed up, but it was them. I heard all about it. Ain't right, beating on a sad old man like that. Lowlife fuckers give criminals a bad name, you know what I'm sayin'?"

"Where are the police?" Gordon asks. "Aren't they investigating?"

"Be serious now. Don't nobody care about no bum."

Rain sprays Gordon's face, drips from the brim of his hat. "Did he die?"

"I heard he on life support or some shit."

"My wife was on life support," Gordon tells him. "Then one night… she died."

The young man's face shows genuine concern. "That's rough, man. But you should go inside, though, all right? Ain't safe on these streets. Go blunt up some of dat fire you got. It take you off to someplace better than all this, you know what I'm sayin'?"

A car appears rather suddenly and rolls to a stop at the mouth of the alley. The dealer hurries over to it, opens the door and looks back at Gordon. He opens his mouth as if he plans to say something else, but apparently thinks better of it, gives a quick wave, then jumps into the car. It speeds off, tires hissing on the wet pavement.

Gordon watches until it disappears into the stormy night. His burned hand throbs painfully, but he focuses instead on the heavy downpour and how it reminds him of the jungle and the way it rained there. Such angry and violent rain, yet it still couldn't wash away all that blood. Blood and death are always stronger. He looks to the corner. The teenagers are on the move.

Gordon follows them.

It has been a very long time since he's hunted, but it all comes back to him with startling clarity. Though there is a chill in the wind and rain, a different kind of cold takes hold of him; one Gordon has kept locked away deep inside and not allowed himself to feel for longer than he can remember. But it is loose now, and moving through him rapidly, transforming him as only it can. Pitiful, weak and frightened old man no more, he is calm and collected, a trained killer moving through the darkness, stalking his prey efficiently and without remorse. He is a ghost, a reaper from the land of the dead, hidden in the rain.

The teens rush down the street, cross at the next corner, then slip into the ruins of a building that was once low-income housing but was largely destroyed and gutted by a fire a few years ago. One of the outer brick walls has collapsed into an enormous pile of rubble, but the other three remain standing and relatively intact, and although the building is condemned, since it still has a roof and can provide at least a certain level of shelter and privacy, it has become an occasional stopover for the neighborhood crack addicts and prostitutes. Gordon has never been inside, but he's walked by many times, and has seen these same teenagers hanging around the building before.

Staying back a fair distance, Gordon tails them. The pain still ravages the small of his back, his shoulders, knees and nearly every joint in his body, and the pain in his injured hand is excruciating, but he no longer cares about any of that. It is no longer relevant, and therefore he cannot allow it to distract, hinder or prevent him from his mission. Just like in the jungle, there is *only* the mission.

He slows his pace, comes to stop across the street from the building. He can see a fire burning inside, giving off enough light that he can make out the silhouettes of the three boys warming themselves around the large metal barrel in which the fire has been set.

This is his jungle now.

Moving through curtains of rain, Gordon crosses the street and slips inside the blown-out first-floor entrance, no longer concerned with stealth as he steps over piles of debris and trash and heads directly for the fire.

The three teens see him immediately, but just stand there, warming their hands and staring at him with looks somewhere between disbelief and indifference. There were five or six teens in the group that attacked the homeless man, but these are three of them. Gordon is sure of it. One is short and stocky; the other two are taller, thinner. None appear to be more than perhaps nineteen.

When Gordon is about ten feet from the barrel, he stops. Standing there dripping, his hands stuffed deep in his raincoat pockets, he stares back at them but says nothing.

"Fuck you want, old man?" the heavyset one finally says.

Gordon takes a step closer, but again, says nothing.

The young men exchange confused glances; then the tallest of the group squares his stance and slowly reaches around to the back of his pants, where presumably he has stashed a weapon of some sort. "You deaf?"

"Probably is," the skinny one chuckles, "old-ass motherfucker."

"What are you doing here?" the tall one asks.

In his coat pocket, Gordon grips the revolver tight. "Do you know who I am?"

"We supposed to know you?" the heavy one asks.

"Hold up." The tall one looks him up and down. "Yeah, I seen you around the neighborhood. You live across from the park."

"That's right," Gordon says. "My windows face the street."

"So?"

"So I saw what you and your friends did this morning."

The teens again exchange uncertain glances. The storm rages just outside, soaking down the city.

"I don't know what the fuck you're talking about," the tall one snaps. "But you need to get out of here and go home before I end your ass. You feel me?"

"No," Gordon says evenly. "I don't feel you at all."'

The other two start toward him, but the tall one stops them with a fierce look. His hand slowly emerges from behind his back. It clutches a 9mm handgun. "What do you want?" he asks. "Fuck you doing here talking shit? You got a death wish or something?"

"I saw what you did to the homeless man." It occurs to Gordon for the first time that he has never learned the man's name, and he is ashamed. *I should know his name*, he thinks. *We should all know his name.* "Did you know he's on life support? You did that to him."

The heavyset boy waves his hands about angrily. "We didn't do shit. Fuck off and get outta here."

"I saw you," Gordon says again.

With the 9mm held down by his leg, the taller boy takes a step closer to Gordon, closing the already small gap between them. "You know who you're playing with? Why you wanna come around here fucking with us?"

"I'm not afraid of you, son."

"I ain't your son."

"Figured you were my grandson."

"Why the hell would you figure that?"

"Because every time I fuck your mother she calls me Daddy."

The other two boys burst out laughing.

"Ba-zing!" the skinny one howls.

The heavyset kid nearly falls over laughing. "You just got served, boy!"

The tall young man doesn't react, and instead appears more baffled than angry or embarrassed. "You crazy? Is that it? You got that *oldzimers* shit or something?" He points the gun at the hole in the wall Gordon entered through. "Go on. I mean it. Get outta here."

"Fuck him, man," the skinny one says, becoming serious again. "Break your foot off in his ass before the stupid bastard calls the cops."

"Ain't nobody gonna listen to this senile fool. Besides, you not about to call the cops, are you?"

"I don't need the police," Gordon assures them. "You do."

The kid narrows his eyes, as if he still can't quite be sure what he's looking at. "You better bounce while you still can, old man."

"Yeah," the heavy one says, "before you go missing your *Matlock* reruns."

The skinny kid laughs as he and his buddy slap hands. "Hurry, it's *Matlock* marathon night, bitch!"

They laugh hysterically, but the tall kid remains serious and calm, his dark eyes locked on Gordon's. "Go home," he says quietly, raising the gun and leveling it at him. "I ain't gonna tell you again."

"Shoot." Gordon slowly leans closer, into the gun, until his right eye comes to rest against the barrel. "Do it. It'll be all right. Just do it. Please."

He holds the 9mm steady, his face a grimace of confusion.

"Please," Gordon whispers.

Gordon…

Gordon can smell the rain, the trash and filth, the shit and piss and sweat, the spent needles and soiled spoons and broken pipes, the empty cans and bottles, the despair, the hopelessness. All his senses are heightened, and he can see and hear and taste and smell like he could years before. "Do you know what I was doing when I was your age?" he asks softly.

Hell in the jungle…firefights and screams…blood and death…

"Do you know what they taught me to do?"

A body pulled from tunnels outside the village…the dirty, bloody, headless torso of a man, the rest of him blown to pieces…Gordon watching as his sergeant yanks the body from the mouth of the tunnel, and holds it up like a trophy, dangling it there for all to see…nearby, an old woman wails in agony and drops to her knees at the sight of her son's remains…

"Do you know what they told me to do?"

The hooch…the fire…the young Vietnamese boy…Gordon holding a gun to his head…demanding things the boy cannot or will not give him…the screams, the chaos, the young man's tears…blood spraying from the boy's temple and his body falling…falling…collapsing into the dirt and dying at Gordon's feet…

"Do you know what I did?"

What have I done? My God, what have I done?

Gordon reaches up with his damaged hand. His fingers, protruding from the tape and towel, gently touch the young man's wrist and push the barrel of the 9mm tighter against his eye socket. "Do it, son."

A shattered mirror…sprayed with blood and pieces of brain and skull…

"Do it."

"Get off me, man!" The kid yanks his hand back, pulling the 9mm from Gordon's face.

I can't make it…

"It was your only chance," Gordon tells him.

"Fuck you talking about?"

In a single fluid motion, Gordon pulls the revolver from his pocket, levels it and fires, shooting him in the center of his forehead.

The discharge is deafening and leaves Gordon's ears ringing, but by the time this registers, he has already pivoted to his left and shot the other two young men, one in the throat and the other in the chest.

Gordon stands there a moment, his gun hand still out in front of him, arm locked, the revolver smoking. Three shots. Three hits. All three young men are on the ground. Two are dead. Only the heavyset one has survived. But he won't live long. Shot in the throat, the bullet has severed his carotid artery, and he writhes about on the ground whimpering, his hands pressed frantically against the wound and already drenched in blood that pumps free of him in unbelievable, cartoonish quantities, soaking his chest and stomach.

Gordon lowers his arm, holds the revolver down by his leg and watches him awhile. "Who do you fear?" he asks flatly. "Who do *you* cry for?"

The kid begins to gag and tries to get to his knees, but flops over onto his back and coughs, spraying blood from his mouth and nose.

Gordon steps closer and shoots him again. This time in the face.

He dies quickly.

After a little while, the buzz in Gordon's ears lessens, and he can hear the rain again. He walks over to the opening in the wall and looks out at the street. It's empty and dark.

He looks back over his shoulder at the three bodies lying around the barrel. The fire continues to burn, pop and spark.

Mr. Cole, this is Dr. Lynch. I regret to inform you that your wife Katharina passed away just a few minutes ago. I'm very sorry for your loss, sir.

Thunder rumbles in the distance.

The ghosts are all around him now, circling, crawling across his skin like insects, whispering their blasphemous inverted prayers as Satan smiles, watching patiently from his throne of human skin and bone.

But Gordon is already gone. The night has swallowed him whole.

EIGHT

The world is an alien landscape now. He is lost and alone. Dead.

But he knows the way. He finds the basement nightclub. Or what was once a nightclub. The sign is gone, replaced by another touting a consignment clothing shop. It sits dark and quiet, as does the rest of the neighborhood, as if everyone and everything has ceased to exist while he's in their midst.

Gordon thinks he hears that angelic singing again, but it's so very far away and sounds sad. It sounds…hopeless…and yet, it stirs something deep within him, begging him closer to…to what? God? Love? Forgiveness? Or something else? Is it a song of hope he hears, or one of sorrow for all that is lost?

"Gordon," Lucy whispers from behind him, wrapping her arms around his waist, then sliding them up across his chest. "I can give you anything you want. Anything. You know that, don't you?"

He knows he will not resist this. He will not resist her. It is meant to be. All of this has been preordained. He convinces himself of this as she kisses and licks his neck, gliding her warm, wet tongue up and into his ear. A chill courses through him, and they fall. Together, they fall.

Around the corner from the Night-Rain Club, in a dirty little motel room most rent by the hour, they collapse onto hard, scratchy sheets that smell like bleach. But Lucy's scent overpowers it all, and Gordon allows it to intoxicate him, even when he realizes what he's really doing, what will really happen.

She tears at his clothes, wrapping her legs tight around his back and locking them at the ankle as she scratches at his bare chest with her blood-red fingernails, begging him to do it, to do it now and everything he has ever wanted will be granted.

Even as he fucks her, Gordon doesn't believe it. He knows, but he doesn't believe it. She is a lost and frightened soul the same as him. Some oversexed woman he picked up at a bar. He tells himself the rest are just thoughts in his head, wishful thinking that will bring Katy to him forever.

"Give her to me," he gasps.

"Will you give yourself to me?"

"Yes."

"Say it."

"I will give myself to you. If you give her to me, I will give myself to you."

As he cums, she screams—ripping into his back with her nails and whispering in his ear what must happen to seal their deal—bucking her hips and taking him deeper as he empties himself inside her.

"I…can't."

"Do it, Gordon. Do it."

He rises up, still inside her, and slowly closes his hands around her throat. "No," she croaks. "There has to be blood."

Gordon raises a fist, closes his eyes, and slams it down into her face…

"Veniat ad me et corpore," *she says, her lip split and already bleeding, running over her chin in glistening crimson. "Come unto me, body and soul."*

"I can't do this, I…"

"Take her heart," Lucy says, only it isn't her voice anymore. It belongs to something else. "Take the little cunt's heart."

Muffled screams echo down a dark corridor.

Gordon backs away, watching the dark stairs that lead down to what is now a consignment shop. He didn't realize it prior, but there is someone down there in the shadows, someone watching. He can hear them laughing.

He crosses the street and hurries off through the rain, knowing now where he must go. He does not look back.

By the time he reaches his old street, the rain has turned to ice and the beginnings of snow. It falls in heavy thick drops that blur his view of the building across the street. But he can see. There, a light on the fourth floor, in the window facing the street. The bedroom, their old bedroom. His and Katy's. It was such a warm and cozy apartment. Katy made it a home—she'd made it *their* home—and now it's all been reduced to memories imprisoned in a tortured mind, teetering on the precipice of madness and damnation.

Halfway down the street is the church Katy attended. A large white cross on its roof glows in the night, through the sleet, a beacon in the otherwise dark night. Gordon reaches inside his shirt and fingers the small gold crucifix he wears on a chain around his neck. It belonged to Katy. He only began wearing it after her death, as a way of having something of hers close to him at all times. He's never expected it to save or protect him, as he's never had much use for such things. He finds comfort in none of the spiritual trinkets so many are fascinated with. It all horrifies him, the good and the bad, the holy and the profane. Where others find power or peace, he finds only chaos, penance and suffering.

He remembers Katy's soft hair against his lips…the taste… the smell…

God, why have you forsaken me?

The quiet. Most of all, he remembers the quiet. Their quiet. Their peace.

Why have I forsaken you?

A car horn blares in the distance, and then an eerie silence returns to the street. Gordon is alone in the icy rain. Sated, the others have faded now, returned to the shadows and retreated into the dark holes from which they crawled.

Do you even exist beyond the piece of you in each of us we call our souls?

Gordon leans against the building for fear he might otherwise collapse onto the sidewalk. He watches the light in the window across the street, hoping to see someone—anyone—but there is only the light.

And then, at the top of the block, a taxi comes to a stop and a man gets out. As the cab pulls away and drives off, Gordon realizes who the man is.

Harry—wrapped tight in a heavy coat, his hat low in front to shield his eyes from the icy rain—hobbles toward him. Having seen Gordon in the shadows, he stops in the street, hands in his coat pockets, like he expects him to say something.

After a moment, Gordon accommodates him. "You shouldn't be here, Harry."

"Neither should you."

"Go away. Go home."

He looks up and down the street, and then up at the apartment window. "I knew I'd find you here," he sighs. "You need to come with me, Gordo. You need to get out of this storm."

"Leave me alone."

Harry notices the bloody towel wrapped and taped around Gordon's arm. "What happened? You're hurt."

"It doesn't matter."

"Look, I—"

"You think I don't know you're in on all of this too?"

Harry shakes his head. "In on all of what?"

"You're the one who recommended Dr. Spires to me."

"I heard he was a good psychiatrist. You needed help, Gordo. You *need* help."

"And he led me to Dr. Amaya. Do you know what Amaya means in Japanese?"

"I haven't the foggiest idea."

"Night Rain."

"And is that supposed to mean something to me?"

"That night, all those years ago. The one we've never talked about. The woman I…I met her at a little joint called the Night-Rain Club."

Harry shuffles his feet in an attempt to ward off the mounting cold. "It's a coincidence, that's all. You're seeing things, making connections and finding conspiracies where there are none."

"No, I—"

"So I'm the enemy now too? *Me?* For Christ's sake, I'm your best friend." He moves a bit closer. "Maybe you've forgotten. I was the one you called that night."

Gordon bows his head. "And I'm sorry, Harry."

"We need to talk about that night. We never have. It's time, Gordo."

"You don't understand."

"No, I'm afraid it's you who doesn't seem to understand. You never have." Harry pushes his hat back a bit, so that Gordon can see his eyes. "You called me that night from the motel, frantic, out of your mind. I'd never heard you like that. Later, when I went there to help you, I'd never seen you in such bad shape. You'd suffered some sort of breakdown, Gordo, you were a wreck."

"I don't want to talk about that night."

"You told me there was a woman, and something terrible had happened. You told me you'd hurt this woman, that you—"

"Stop it, Harry!"

"That you'd killed this woman, that you—"

"Stop!" Gordon pushes away from the building, joins Harry in the street.

"You said you'd killed her. You'd beaten her to death and torn her heart from her chest and that you'd done it to be with Katy, that it was some sort of twisted satanic ritual or some similar nonsense." Harry reaches out, puts his hands on Gordon's shoulders. "Gordon, you were out of your mind. You said the body was in the bed, that the entire room was covered in blood, and that you needed me to help you clean the place up and dispose of the body."

"Harry—"

"Only there was no body. There was no blood. There was only you and I in an empty motel room."

"She said her name was Lucy, don't you see? A sick joke. Lucy—Lucifer, Harry—*Lucifer*, it was all a demented and evil joke, a—"

"There was no Lucy, Gordon. You didn't hurt anyone that night but yourself. The room was mussed, you'd had some sort of violent episode, but there was no one else there, no blood and no body. I helped you straighten the place up and we got out of there."

Gordon stares into his old friend's eyes. Is this true? *Could* it be?

"We got the hell out of there and we never spoke of it again," Harry tells him. "You were suffering, still battling your demons from the war, and you'd met Katy by then and wanted her desperately. You were in love, and you were terrified of losing her. You'd found someone, for the first time in your life you'd found someone who made you truly happy, someone who made you feel…normal. Within weeks, you and Katy were together and happy, there was no need to revisit that night. It didn't matter. Not then, not now."

Come unto me…

Gordon turns, takes a few steps away. He is so tired, so confused and weak, so cold and wet. "I…I only wanted Katy, I…"

"Gordo, listen to me. Katy was the best thing that ever happened to you. You had something with her most of us can only dream about, and you had it a long time. When she got sick, you fell apart, and I understand, I—I would've too. But a part of you has never forgiven her. It was her choice, Gordon. It was *her* choice."

"She used my gun," he says softly.

You lied to me.

"She didn't want to suffer, to waste away. She didn't want you to have to see her suffer and go on and on until she died. Katy never meant for you to find her. It was the middle of the day I'm sure she thought someone would hear the shot and call the police."

Of course…

"I sold my soul, Harry. I sold my soul to the Devil to have her."

"Listen to yourself. There was no woman, Gordon. And there is no Devil. All there is are two lonely and broken-down old men in the rain."

"I…I miss her, Harry, I…" Gordon feels the emotion welling up in him again, but stronger this time, the strongest it's ever been, and he can no longer control it. The wall implodes, taking the cold with it, ripping it all away to raw bone.

Finally unleashed, the tears refuse to stop.

"I miss her so much."

Harry puts a hand on his shoulder. "I know, mate. But it's

going to be all right. We're going to get you some help and it'll be all right."

"I don't want to live without her, I—what the fuck am I still doing here? I'm a ridiculous old man just marking time and—I never deserved her, Harry, I never deserved her and—I drew her into this mess, into me and my fucked-up life, and she paid for it, and now I can't—I can't forgive myself, Harry, I *can't*, I—"

"It'll be all right." Harry draws him closer, hugging him from behind. "It'll be all right. Just hang on, Gordo, you have to hang on and get your head straight."

Gordon cries for a very long time, the tears hitting in waves of wailing sobs that wrack his entire body. When it finally softens, Harry slowly lets him go, and Gordon turns and faces him, able to look him in the eye again. "Something horrible happened tonight," he tells him. "Those boys who attacked the homeless man. I…"

Harry says nothing, waits for him to finish.

Instead, Gordon pulls the revolver from his coat pocket and shows it to him.

"What have you done?" he asks.

"There are two bullets left."

"One for each of us, eh?" Harry's face hints at a sad smile. There seem to be no other kind on this night.

Something distracts him. They're back. He can hear them just above the din of rainfall. "The angels," Gordon mumbles, "they…they're singing again. Can you hear them, Harry? Can you hear them too, if you listen very hard?"

"Let's go home, Gordon. Let's get out of here and go home."

"Home to what?"

Gordon wipes his eyes with the back of his hand, and holding the revolver down by his side, wanders over to the curb and slowly sinks down until he's sitting on the edge of it. After a moment, Harry joins him.

They sit there for some time, neither saying a word.

The icy rain gradually turns to snow, and quiet returns to the city, as big fat soundless flakes swirl and tumble about, coating the street and buildings quickly. Even here, even on this night, there is beauty.

Harry pulls a flask from his coat pocket, takes a pull, then offers it to Gordon.

The angels' voices fade.

Gordon takes a long drink. The whiskey burns his throat, warms him as it travels down. He hands the flask back, watches the light in the window. "You deserved to be loved," Harry tells him. "We all deserve to be loved. And you had it for a very long time. But nothing lasts forever, Gordo. Nothing. No one."

"Do I, Harry? Did I?" The gun is cold in his hand. "I'm a bad man."

"You're *just* a man," Harry corrects him. "Nothing more, nothing less."

"I don't want to live anymore. But I'm afraid to die."

"We're all afraid to die. It's why we fight so hard to live. Who knows what's on the other side?"

Gordon wipes snow, or perhaps more tears, from his eyes. "I do."

Harry takes another drink. "Maybe those angels you hear… maybe they're singing for you."

"Lucifer was an angel. Some say the most beautiful of all the angels."

"Why not? There's a fine line between beauty and horror, and nothing at all between light and dark."

"There's us," Gordon says. "*We're* between the light and the dark."

Snow continues to fall across the city.

Harry offers him the flask again. "Another pop?"

"Go home, Harry. You should go home."

"I'm not going anywhere."

Gordon takes the flask, drinks.

"Did you call the police before you came looking for me?"

Harry nods.

"Did you tell them where I was?"

"I gave them a couple options. This was one."

"Then they'll be here soon."

"Yes."

"Do they know what I've done?"

Harry takes the flask back and tucks it into his coat, but never answers.

The light in the apartment window goes out. Shadows on the street shift and conform. At the corner, the snow dances in the only surviving light, a pool of it cast from a street lamp. The flakes look as if they're alive. In a way, they are.

"Two bullets left," Gordon reminds him.

"Why don't you give me the gun?"

"You know I can't do that."

"I only know you won't."

"I'm not going back, Harry."

"I know."

"I can't run anymore."

"That's because you can't outrun yourself, Gordo." Harry's face, bathed in shadow and snowflakes, creases in pain. "There's no one else chasing you."

Who do you cry for?

"There is a devil nipping at your heels, Gordon, but it's you."

Who do you fear?

"It's the devil in you, Gordon. The devil in all of us."

There are no sirens, only lights. Blue lights that cut the darkness and snow, whirling round and round, illuminating the buildings in quick swathes that glide past at lightning speed, gone then back again. Gordon looks to his old apartment window, waits for the lights to pass.

"There's…someone there," he says. "Watching us."

"Please, Gordon. Put the gun down."

With great effort, Gordon struggles back to his feet, his eyes locked on the window. Another pass of blue light, and he again sees a silhouette. Someone is watching him from the dark apartment.

"Katy?" he asks, moving into the center of the street. "Katy, is it…is it you?"

Slowly, the black form in the window opens its arms… spreads its black, leathery wings…

Who do you fear?

"No…" Gordon looks away, to the end of the street. The lights, so beautiful in their own way, so alive… moving rhythmically across his face and body now…

Gordon…

The angels, asleep in their house of rain, no longer sing for him. Or perhaps he just can't hear them anymore.

Gordon…

Perhaps he's no longer meant to.

Who do you cry for?

Perhaps they sing for someone else now.

Gordon…

Perhaps they always have.

The lights…like a prism…the snowflakes…like butterflies burned to ash…and the dead…they're there too…

"I'm so tired, Katy, I…so tired." Tears and snow stream across his cold, flushed cheeks. "It's too late, isn't it? It's always been too late."

"Why don't you sit here awhile with me?" she says, smiling at him from the curb. "And we'll see?"

Only it's not Katy at all, it is just Harry sitting there, sweet and loyal Harry, with that same sad and silly grin on his face.

But it's all right. It's all he has on this cold wintery night. And it's enough. He knows this now. It's enough.

He drops down onto the curb with a muffled grunt. From the corner of his tear-blurred vision, he sees the lights, so full and bright, so close, and swears there are others within those lights. Waiting. Waiting for him.

"Yes," he says, looking up once more to the dark apartment window, the gun cold and heavy in his hand. "Let's just sit here awhile and see."

He returned his attention to the street below, the lights and the two men sitting on the curb.

"What's happening?" his wife asked.

"Bunch of police cars out there, and there are two men down on the curb across the street." He returned to bed, sat on the edge. "Whatever they've done, it must be pretty bad to warrant five cruisers. I'll be careful, but I need to see what's happening."

She nods, coughs.

"I don't like the sounds of that cough."

She nods again, rubs her chest.

"What's wrong, sweetheart?"

"Not feeling well. Just don't feel right. So tired all the time, and this cough."

"You're awfully pale lately," he said, placing a hand on her shoulder. "You'd better make an appointment with the doctor."

"Already have. I'm sure it's nothing serious."

He put his arms around her, drew her to him and hugged her tight. As he closed his eyes, somewhere out in that dark and snowy night, he could've sworn he heard singing...

House of Rain the most beautiful singing he had ever heard in his life.

"I think they're gone, love."

Gordon...

He opened his eyes. The lights were no longer sweeping across their bedroom walls. "Yes," he whispered. Letting her go, he returned to the window. There was nothing out there but a dark night, and a beautiful snowfall slowly covering the city. *We're just pretending, aren't we?*

There's no way out.

"What is it?" Katy asked. "Gordon, are you all right?"

We're living on borrowed time. But isn't everyone?

She joined him at the window, wrapping her arms around his waist and resting her chin on his shoulder. "What's wrong, sweetheart? You're trembling."

Who do you fear?

"Nothing, just a little cold, I guess."

"Look at it out there." She hugged him tighter. "It's just so beautiful, isn't it?"

He wondered if she could hear what he was hearing. A part of him hoped so.

"Do you think the snow will stop anytime soon?" she asked.

Gordon let himself fall back into her, and the warmth and love of her arms. "Let's hope not," he said quietly. "Let's hope not."

LORDS OF TWILIGHT

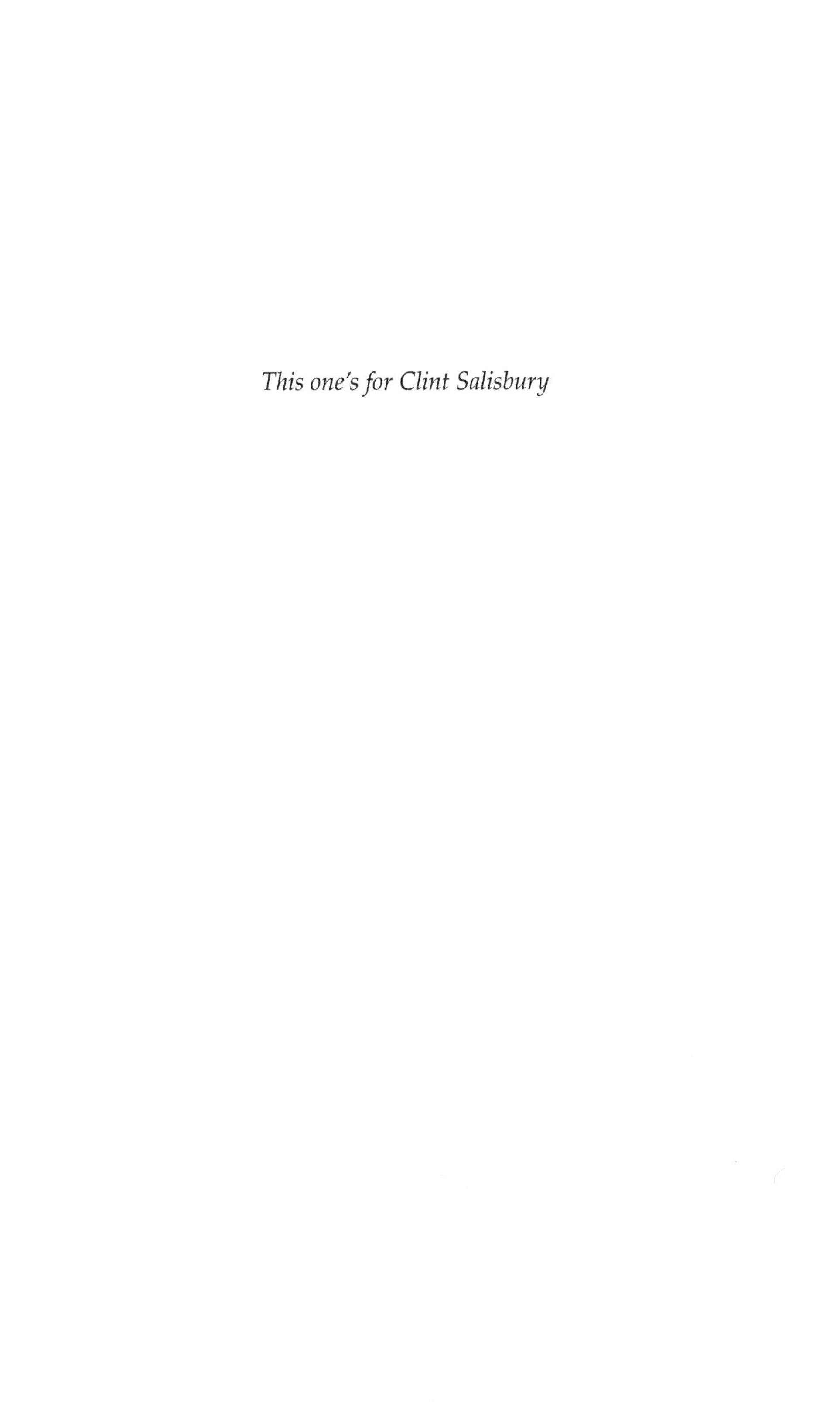

This one's for Clint Salisbury

"Two possibilities exist: Either we are alone in the Universe or we are not. Both are equally terrifying."

—Arthur C. Clarke

ONE

The girl does not run. Through clouds of breath he sees her standing in the center of the snowy road, still as a mannequin and staring straight at him with hollow black sockets where her eyes should be. In a winter world of endless white, the dark craters look like pools of ink mistakenly spilled on an otherwise pallid canvas. The nightmare is dying, decaying right before him, returning to the shadowy lies of night from which they came. Around them, on this desolate wooded road, the storm is over but renegade snowflakes still fly about in the delicate light of early morning.

But for his labored breath, it is eerily silent.

A whimpering sound behind him draws his attention. He glances back quickly at the puppy trembling near a snow bank on the side of the road. "It's OK," he says, his voice gravelly and strained, foreign as it echoes across the frozen landscape. "Stay there."

He turns toward the girl. She still hasn't moved. She won't. He knows this now. There is nowhere else to go, and like him, she—it—is weakening.

A gust of icy wind cuts through him like a razor.

Despite his pain and exhaustion, he summons a primal screech he hopes will silence the tempest of demonic whispers slithering through his head, and raising the ax, staggers forward along the road. Emma opens her arms in welcome, even as he stumbles closer and slams the blade down into the top of her skull.

Even then, he knew they were watching. He didn't know how or why or even what *they* were, but he knew there were eyes on him. Eyes that could peer deep inside him where all those things he didn't want anyone to see crawled to darkness and hid away. He could feel it. He could feel *them*. But it all seemed little more than a dream, really, a vague premise drifting through an exhausted mind. The possibility that something was *out there* but on its way to him, or perhaps had already arrived, he couldn't be certain either way, refused to leave him. All he knew for sure was that he was no longer alone with his thoughts and fears. Something else had joined him in these things. Something sinister.

"For God's sake," he sighed, "get hold of yourself."

Even before the storm most of the locals had been spooked, but Lane knew better than to allow such foolishness to frighten him or cloud his judgment. He had no doubt his feelings of paranoia were a subconscious reaction to the goings on in town of late, yet they remained impossible to dismiss.

It all began about a week before, when three cows from one of the farms in town had turned up missing, only to be found hours later strewn across an open field like discarded garbage. The carcasses had been mutilated, with wounds which appeared to be precision cuts, many of them burned into the animal's flesh, as if some sort of laser tool or high-tech scalpel had been used. According to the local newspaper, the animals' sexual organs had been removed, along with their rectal areas, eyes and mouths. These sorts of things had been reported before, but never in or even near Edgar, and as rumors swept through town like wildfire, blaming the mutilations on everything from satanic cults to drugged-out teenagers to space aliens to shady government agents, the tension in town grew worse. When within days, a handful of people reported seeing strange lights in the skies, things only got worse.

There's a reasonable explanation, he thought. *And if I believe anything different I may as well buy into the theory that garden gnomes are responsible.*

The swirl of snowflakes caught his attention, mesmerizing him as they had since childhood. He watched the ribbons of snow fall gracefully from the gray sky, spiraling toward Earth in beautiful twirling garlands, the newborn flakes riding the wind before exploding into bursts of powdery dust. There was only an inch or two of accumulation but the weather reports had called for close to two feet before the storm was said and done. Lane knew he couldn't be long. He had to get home while the roads were still passable.

His old pickup shimmied and rattled as he pulled it up an incline and onto the property he'd been told about. Perhaps forty yards ahead was a rundown shack of a house, interchangeable with any number of others sprinkled throughout these woods and lonely back roads. He'd driven by the place a few times but had never stopped. Now that he had, he still wasn't certain he'd have the guts to get out and go through with this.

Lane saw the man's breath first, tumbling from him in smoky plumes. Tall and rugged, with a shabby salt-and-pepper beard and dark eyes, he was already ambling toward Lane's truck, a bloody machete slung over his shoulder. Behind the man, a partially skinned deer carcass hung in the open doorway of a garage to the right of the house. Lane gave a quick glance over at Vince, his little lab puppy that was white as the falling snow. The dog was sound asleep, so Lane pushed open the driver's side door and hopped out of the truck. The smell of innards and death—the kill—filled the air, but it was so cold out it quickly dissipated. He was glad he'd kept his sunglasses on. Nerves had left him a bit lightheaded, and daylight reflecting off the snowy ground cast the area in an otherworldly glow, making everything much brighter than inside the truck. He pulled his coat in tight around him.

"Morning."

"Surely is that," the man said.

"Are you Mr. Snead?"

"A-yah." He slowed his stride but kept coming. "I know you?"

"We've never met. Clyde Reeve suggested I come and see you."

"Did he now?" Snead finally came to a stop a few feet from him.

"Yes, sir, he did."

"Clyde Reeve I know. You I don't."

"I'm Lane Boyce."

Snead scratched at his knit hat with the battered fingers of a man who had spent his life laboring with his hands. "You that *New Yawk* boy?"

No one had called Lane a boy in a very long time. He'd recently turned forty-seven, which probably made him somewhere in the vicinity of ten years younger than Snead. "Boston, actually."

"*Baston,* right." Snead squinted as if he'd suddenly lost sight of him. "Ya been in town a while now, seen ya around."

"Going on seven months, moved here the beginning of May."

"Ya livin' up to Freddy Tate's place."

"Well it's my place now, but yes. I bought it from Mr. Tate's widow."

He jerked a thumb back at the deer carcass. "Lookin' to buy some venison, are ya?"

"Not today."

Snead sucked air through the gaping space between his front teeth, wiped a trickle of snot from his nostril with the back of his hand and gazed out at the snow-covered trees along the backside of the property.

"Somethin' else then?"

"Yes."

"Half hour do ya?"

"Yes, that—that's fine."

"Fifty *dollahs,* cash in hand."

Lane pulled two twenties and a ten from his wallet and gave them to him, hopeful Snead hadn't seen his hands shaking.

The big man motioned to the shack with his chin then turned and started back toward the deer remains. When he looked over his shoulder and saw that Lane hadn't moved, he chuckled. "Well go on then, what ya waitin' for? Clock's a-tickin'."

Lane crossed the yard, climbed two rickety steps then hesitated before the closed front door. He glanced over at Snead, who gestured for him to go ahead, so he turned the knob and stepped directly into a filthy and cluttered kitchen, the table covered with old mail, empty beer and liquor bottles, coffee mugs, drug paraphernalia, a box of Frosted Flakes and a plate stained with egg yolk. The house was cramped, dusty and old, a basic box. Nothing looked as if it had been cleaned in months. Beyond the kitchen was a small den area outfitted with a threadbare couch and an old rocking chair. A ragamuffin of a little girl sat on the floor doodling in a coloring book, a box of crayons spilled about her. In the far corner a potbelly woodstove crackled, filling the house with thick, oppressive heat. Clad in a robe and slippers, the little girl looked up at Lane through a curtain of matted hair and smiled. His heart broke for her. She couldn't have been more than five or six. Masking his true emotions, Lane smiled and waved hello. She waved back then returned to her coloring book. *What in God's name am I doing here?* With a sigh, he moved through the kitchen and into a short hallway. At the end stood a bathroom, the door open, and to his right was a bedroom, a string of beads hanging in the doorway.

Moving the beads aside with one hand, Lane ducked through and into a tiny bedroom. Everything smelled vaguely of pipe tobacco laced with body odor. Lane removed his sunglasses and gave his eyes a moment to adjust to the relatively dark room: A bed, a bureau, and a small washbasin on the floor. The only window was outfitted with thick plastic sheeting rather than glass, and the scarred plank floor was bare, as were the walls. Propped in the corner was a large wooden crucifix that looked as if it had been left there mistakenly.

On the edge of the mussed and unmade bed sat a woman in a full slip, a cardigan sweater tossed over her shoulders. Petite and shockingly thin, her bare feet just barely touched the floor. Her toenails were painted circus red but the polish was chipped and fading, and her skinny legs were littered with bruises and scrapes. Her brown hair was a rat's nest held off her shoulders with a plastic clip, and her eyes were dull and heavily made up with black shadow and liner, causing her already pale complexion to appear even starker. "I'm Marla," she said, sounding and looking as if she'd just awakened from a deep sleep.

He cleared his throat. "Hello."

"Can always tell the ones who never done this before."

Emma's face drifted past his mind's eye, her lips breaking into a smile as she whispered to him from the past. *You've never done this before, have you?*

Marla gave a wry smile. "Relax, it ain't nothin'."

As the memory of Emma thankfully retreated to the darkness from which she'd come, Lane tried to estimate Marla's age. She bore the decaying and haggard look of a longtime meth addict, so it was hard to know for sure. His best guess was she was somewhere in her late thirties to early forties.

She stifled a yawn. "How much time you got?"

"Thirty minutes."

"How you want to spend it?"

He stood there stupidly, unsure of what to do or say.

"It's OK, you can tell me. Don't be shy." She reached for a pack of cigarettes on the bureau, shook one free and rolled it into the corner of her mouth. "I've heard it all and done most of it, ain't like you're gonna shock me."

"I don't want sex," he told her.

"Say again?"

"Sex, I…I don't want sex."

"Well darlin' that's what I'm selling." She plucked a disposable lighter from her ample cleavage and fired up the cigarette. "Hell's wrong with you? Whatcha lookin' to buy, furniture?"

Lane fought the urge to leave, though he wasn't entirely sure why. "All I really want is some of your time."

Marla drew a deep drag on her cigarette and exhaled through her nose. "OK."

"I thought maybe we could just sit together a while." Even as he said it he realized how pathetic it sounded. Lane's face flushed and he looked down at the floor. How had his life come to this?

"So…you just wanna look and jack-off or somethin'?"

"No, nothing like that," he said, voice shaking. "I'd just like to sit here with you. We don't even have to talk if you don't want to."

She puffed her cigarette, sizing him up through vines

of smoke slowly climbing toward the ceiling. "That's all," he added. "That's all I want."

"You don't even want to talk dirty or nothin'?"

"I'm sorry," he said, turning back to the beads, "I shouldn't have come, I—"

"You the one that bought the Tate place?"

Lane looked back, nodded. "You all alone out there?"

"I have a dog."

"The Tate place, shit, talk about the middle of nowhere in the middle of nowhere." She sniffled, wiped her nose and flicked cigarette ash on the floor. "You ain't married or got a girlfriend or nothin'?"

"I've been divorced about a year and a half now."

"How long was you married?"

"Twenty years."

"Long-ass time."

"Yes it is."

"Almost fifteen for me."

"Congratulations."

"Your wife run off on ya, did she?"

"No. It was my fault."

"You don't got no kids?"

Normally he would've found such questions intrusive, but they distracted him from his embarrassment at having gone there in the first place so he made no objections. "No."

She pondered his response a while. "How come?"

It never ceased to amaze him how people had no qualms asking such a personal question once they learned he was without children. Didn't it occur to them there might be any number of reasons, and none of them their business?

"We tried twice when we were younger but my wife miscarried both times," he explained. "After the second pregnancy failed we decided not to try again."

"Oh. Sorry. Really, I am."

"It was a long time ago."

Snow ticked against the plastic sheet covering the window.

"Lot of weird shit happenin' in town, you heard about it?"

He nodded.

"Some say the end of the world's coming, judgment day and all that. Bad for business, makes everybody run to church, try to save their ass before it's too late. But they'll be back. Only time sinners ain't sinnin' is when they're scared, and don't nobody stay scared forever." She took a pull on her cigarette. "You think that shit's for real? Judgment Day and all that?"

"I sure hope not."

With a slight smile, Marla dropped her cigarette into the washbasin on the floor. It died with a quick hiss. "Come on over here and sit down with me."

Lane did. The bed was so soft and worn he could feel the springs digging into the backs of his legs. Up close, Marla smelled like she'd just had sex in an ashtray, but there was something in her sad eyes he felt connected to. She took his hands in hers and gave them a gentle squeeze. Her skin was slightly damp.

"How long's it been since somebody put their arms around you?"

Rather than answer, Lane let his head rest on her shoulder. She brought her free hand around, pulled him close and held him tight. Despite his shame and embarrassment, he melted into her as tears filled his eyes, and even when the world became a wet and blurry mess, he did not let go.

The ride back was treacherous, but he and Vince arrived safely. Lane shut the engine off, sat in silence and watched the house through the steadily falling snow. This place still didn't feel like home to him and probably never would. That had become a concept just beyond his reach it seemed, a memory of another place and time he could never return to. Like so much else, it was gone and he'd never get it back. The house was quite small, a squat weathered structure amidst seventeen acres of woodland. A single-story, one-bedroom with a modest front porch and a hand-dug cellar, it was originally built in the late 1930s, and until Lane took ownership, had belonged to the same local family for decades. Even for such a rural and scarcely populated town as Edgar (a burgh of less than five hundred residents located in northern Maine), his property was, as Marla had said, the middle of nowhere in the middle of nowhere. The town proper was more than five miles away and consisted of only a few stores, a post office, town hall and a one-engine firehouse (Edgar didn't even have its own police department, and fell under the jurisdiction of the state police, the closest barracks being miles away). More than two miles separated Lane from his nearest neighbor, an older couple he'd never met or spoken to. Many nearby areas didn't even have names. They were simply numbers on maps where people still lived with generator-driven electricity or none at all, and often little to no indoor plumbing. Things weren't quite that primitive in Edgar, however. Lane had electric, a woodstove for heat, and indoor plumbing. Most of it even worked on a regular basis. But modern technology was scarce. He didn't even own a television. He'd planned on buying one once he moved in but with no cable or satellite service available and only a roof antenna there seemed little point. And there was no cellphone reception in Edgar either, so his only real connection to the outside world was his landline telephone. That and his laptop, which he rarely used and even then only for basic Internet and email use (provided his antiquated dial-up connection felt like working). Mostly he read or listened to music or news on a portable radio, and although being detached from technology and the world at large was a difficult adjustment at first, Lane was surprised how little he missed it and how quickly he'd become accustomed to living without it.

He looked to the small outbuilding perhaps fifty yards behind and slightly to the left of the house. Not quite big enough for more than a single automobile but considerably larger than a standard shed, he'd spent two full days that summer cleaning it out and driving mountains of junk to the dump only to realize he had nothing of his own to put in there save for some assorted tools, a lawnmower, a generator, a rake and a couple shovels. A large portion of the storage building sat empty, much like Lane himself, awaiting things that would more than likely never arrive. Both buildings were draped in growing blankets of snow and set back far enough from the road that one could easily drive past without noticing them at all. But for the smoke drifting up out of the woodstove chimney, just barely visible through the swirling snow, there were no immediate indications anyone even lived there.

With the heater off it was quickly growing cold in the cab. In the seat next to him, Vince lay with his chin resting on Lane's thigh, eyes gazing up at him questioningly. Only three months old, he'd gotten him at six weeks from a small breeder down in Bangor for nine hundred dollars. Lane loved animals but hadn't had a dog or cat in years because his ex-wife suffered from pet dander allergies. After moving to Edgar and buying the house, Lane had spent nearly five months alone. Given the circumstances that had brought him there, that arrangement initially suited him just fine. He'd wanted isolation, quiet and privacy, that's why he'd come here after all, but winters were brutal in these parts, and the thought of spending all those months alone was less than appealing. Although he spent most of his downtime drinking and wallowing in his sorrows and was in no position to care for an animal, that lifestyle had quickly worn thin and he decided he needed companionship. A dog seemed a good choice, as he'd always liked dogs and had several as a child. Besides, he needed a change in his life that would force him to be more responsible and clearheaded. He also needed someone to love, someone to love him and someone to take care of and occupy his time, and a puppy certainly fit the bill. He and Vince bonded quickly, and though he'd only had the puppy a little over a month, Lane already couldn't imagine life without him. He reached down and gave him a gentle pat on the head. "Come on, bud," he said softly. "Let's go inside and get warm."

TWO

Three. Three fingers where once there were five.

His hand is obscene, mangled and stained black. The cold does awful things to the flesh. He stares at it as if noticing it only just then, watching as the odd gelatinous fluid drips from his surviving fingers, falling and splatting on the floor below in thick heavy gobs. What is this clear though copious, jelly-like substance coating so much of him? For reasons beyond his comprehension, he is unable to remember how or why his injuries came to be. It isn't until he looks in the mirror on the wall and sees the damage his face has sustained that he begins to remember being in the snow and how the bitter ice and cold ate through his skin right to the bone. He considers touching the black and cracked caterpillars that were once his lips, the crusted sores on his cheeks and around his eyes, but thinks better of it.

Something tickles his nose. With his good hand he reaches up and touches his nostrils. Blood. So much, too much, it runs down between his fingers to the palm of his hand.

And then in the mirror behind him he sees…something.

What is *that?*

A bird, it—it's a bird, a blackbird. It's enormous, he thinks, perched there at the window on the far wall, its opaque eyes glaring at him.

Somewhere in the distance he hears a dog barking.

His dog? Is it his dog?

He turns from the mirror and moves slowly toward the window, heart racing, though he has no idea why.

Lane grabbed two pieces of cut wood from a bin tucked between the kitchen table and the refrigerator and dropped them into the woodstove. Using a poker, he stabbed at the pieces he'd dropped in earlier, which had been reduced to red-hot chunks that spit sparks as he shuffled them around to make room for the new. Heat wafted up into his face, drying his eyes. He glanced down at Vince, who sat at his feet, tail gently slapping the floor. "I've got it going really strong now," he told the dog. "Be nice and warm in here in no time." Apparently pleased with the news, Vince toddled over to his little toy basket in the corner, plucked out a squeaky chew toy shaped like a duck then curled up with it next to the table. Lane watched the pup a while, marveling at how happy the little fella was. He envied him, really, and could only hope he'd experience true happiness again himself some day. But then, maybe it was better that happiness continued to elude him (save for those brief and infrequent episodes that seemed to manifest as if mistakenly). Maybe, he thought, I don't deserve it anyway.

Hands on hips, Lane took in the kitchen a moment. With its dated countertops, cabinets and meager appliances, the whole place looked like something from another era, which, in a way, it was. Due to low wood-slat ceilings and small rooms, the house was always a bit dark. Sometimes it felt warm and cozy, other times claustrophobic, cold and coffin-like. On that morning, with the blizzard approaching, it seemed more like the latter, an old wooden casket destined to be buried beneath foot after foot of snow he could never hope to escape. He thought for a moment. Did he have everything he needed? Once the storm got into full swing the very real possibility of being snowed in for a few days was not something to take lightly. He'd gone to the General Store in town and gotten the necessities but went over the list again in his head, taking inventory in an attempt to be sure he hadn't forgotten anything. The mudroom, a small area with a cement floor and a broom closet just inside the front door, housed the larger woodbin. He checked it again. Though nearly full, his experience with woodstoves was limited and he had no idea how to correctly gauge how much he'd need or go through over a given period of time. Looked like an awful lot of wood in there, though, could he really go through that in three or four days should he become so snowed in that he couldn't get to the outbuilding and the piles of wood Clyde Reeve had cut for him? Lane moved to the window, looked out at the growing storm. Even if they got the two feet the news reports claimed were coming, it's not like he couldn't get out. Right? *Hmmm,* he thought. *Not like anyone's going to be plowing. At least not right away.* Clyde did say he'd be by to plow soon as he could once the storm had gone, but 'soon' had one definition to Lane and another to those living in these parts. Time was slower here, and folks moved through their lives accordingly, without the frenetic sense of urgency city people often wore like a badge of honor. It was a trait Lane found irritating and admirable all at once. He could almost hear his old friend and colleague Russell complaining as he had when he'd come up for a visit just weeks after Lane arrived in town.

"OK, so how long before the inbred family of hillbilly cannibals shows up?"

"Russell, seriously, what the hell is wrong with you?"

"You move to this swill-hole and you're asking what's wrong with *me*?"

Russell had done his best to try and talk Lane out of moving to Maine, and even after he'd purchased the house and moved in, he made one last valiant attempt to convince him to move back to Boston.

"I understand the desire—hell, the need—to get away to a place where no one knows you or cares who you are," he'd said, "somewhere you can have the quiet and uncomplicated life of a hermit. After everything that happened, I get it, OK? I don't agree with it, I don't think it's what you need or what's best for you, but I get it. But *here*? Seriously? I've never even heard of this town."

"I hadn't either," Lane admitted. "I just told the real estate agent I wanted a property somewhere remote and this is what she came up with."

"I take it there was nothing available on the moon?"

"It suits my needs for now."

"What needs would those be?"

"Look, I picked this place up for just over fifty thousand

dollars. I couldn't buy a closet in Boston for fifty grand."

"I've had car loans that were more than that. What does that tell you?"

"No mortgage, no hassles."

"No people with teeth or reading skills, no running toilets, no resale value."

Lane chuckled dutifully. "It's not so bad. Honestly, it isn't. It's quiet and secluded and no one bothers me."

"What the hell do you do up here?"

"There isn't a whole lot to do. That's the point."

"And what do you plan to do for work?"

"Claire and I got a little over three for the apartment and had close to thirty in savings. After we paid the remainder of the mortgage and our other bills off and the lawyers on both sides took their cuts there was two hundred thousand left to split between us. Fifty bought this property and I put the rest in the bank and into various investments. I'm OK for a while."

Russell Brunel, a short and rugged man with thinning hair and a penchant for wrinkled sports coats, faded jeans and ratty sneakers, looked more like a retired fullback than the high school teacher Lane knew him to be. In fact, in his own high school days Russell had been a star athlete on both the football and wrestling teams, but neither had panned out beyond college and he'd fallen back on his teaching degree instead. He and Lane had met and become friends when both were hired within a few months of each other at the same small prep school in Boston. Until Lane's difficulties, they'd both worked there for more than two decades, Lane in the English Department, Russell in Math. Though they were the same age, Russell was long divorced and had remained a bachelor ever since, somehow managing to regularly bed most of the female teachers on staff and half the women in the administration office. "And what about your career?"

"My career's over."

"You don't ever plan to return to teaching?"

"I don't know."

"It's not as if you *couldn't*." He cleared his throat awkwardly. "I mean the option does still exist if—"

"Would you go back? If you were me, Russ, would you?"

"You know my philosophy. Long as the little bastards keep showing up somebody's got to get paid to be there and teach them, might as well be me." He scratched his goatee with a big mitt of a hand. "I do it because I can't make a living doing anything else. You teach because you genuinely love it and it's a part of who you are. You did it for all the right reasons." He shook his head as an expression of disgust crossed his face. "Talk about irony."

"Well, at this point I don't know what I'm doing, but I seriously doubt I'll ever go back, OK?"

"Sure." Russell had known him long enough to read his tone, and thankfully let it go. "OK."

"Let's go have some lunch," Lane suggested.

"So around here that entails what, killing a bear or something?"

"There's a decent diner about thirty minutes from here, wiseass."

"Thirty minutes to eat at a diner. Awesome."

"It gets worse. It's forty to the nearest liquor store."

Russell stared at him, mouth open in mock horror.

"Come on," Lane said, "let me buy you some lunch."

But even once the joking was over, Russell remained seated. "Before we go I have to get this off my chest. I'm sorry if I'm being a d-bag but this is just plain creepy. You all alone up here in the middle of nowhere in this little house in the woods, it's not right. Time like this you need to be around people who care about you, not all by yourself. And do you have any idea what the winters are like this far north? You think Boston's cold? People die in this shit up here."

"I'll be all right."

"I guess I just don't see the point. Why not move in with me for a while? I've got plenty of room and I'd love to have you."

"I appreciate it, Russ, I really do. But we've been over this. I'm not suggesting I'll be here forever, but for now this is what I need to do."

"What, run away and hide?"

"Yes," he said quietly. "At least for now."

Russell sat forward and gripped the edge of the kitchen table with both hands, as if fearful he might otherwise begin pounding it with his fists. "Goddamn travesty what they did to you."

Guilt rose in Lane like bile bubbling up into the base of his throat. Per usual, it brought shame along for the ride. "Let's not go there, all right?"

"I'm just saying, it was—"

"Did you come here to cheer me up and hang out or give me a hard time?"

"I see no reason why I can't do both."

Neither man seemed capable of summoning laughter, so they forced a couple smiles instead. "I know you don't like what I'm doing," Lane finally said. "I'm not entirely sure I do either. All I do know is that I need some time away and some time alone."

"I'm just concerned about you."

"And I appreciate it. But I'll be fine. This is something I need to do, Russ."

He released the table and rose to his feet. "Just wait until winter hits. Mark my words. You'll dig out and have this place on the market the same day."

His old friend's face faded into oblivion, replaced by the dimly lit kitchen. He'd spoken to Russell on the telephone several times but hadn't laid eyes on him since. Due to the school year, the odds of seeing him at any point before next summer were remote at best. But Thanksgiving was only a few weeks away, and then the Christmas season would be in full swing, and he knew Russell would insist he accompany him to his sister's house in his native New Jersey for the holiday break. Of course Lane had no plans to do any such thing. The way he figured it, by the following summer he'd have had enough time to ponder his past, present and future and be ready to make some decisions. Either he'd remain where he was and live out a solitary life as best he could, or he'd get the hell out of Dodge and start over again somewhere else. Regardless, until then, this was his home, his prison, and hopefully his penance.

Suddenly Lane had an overwhelming need to look outside.

Perplexed, he moved closer to the window and peered up at the snow-draped treetops and low dark clouds beyond.

So many places to hide…

Where had *that* thought come from? Before he could answer his own question the feeling that he was being watched took hold and clamped down on him like a vise. He'd been experiencing on-again off-again intervals of this for a few days now, and although like everyone else he'd had similar feelings before at various points in his life, these episodes were different, more profound. Darker.

Snow whipped between the trees. Lane's eyes followed, searching the narrow spaces between them, but visibility had already become limited. *Nothing out there but a whirl of snowflakes anyway,* he thought. He ran a hand through his hair, drew a deep breath and let it out slowly. What was this all about? He'd never felt spooked here before, or even the least bit uncomfortable. Why then was he suddenly so uneasy? True, this was his first winter as far north as Edgar, but Lane was a native New Englander; he'd been through numerous snowstorms and several blizzards in his life, they neither intimidated nor frightened him.

Of course the cattle mutilations and stories of lights in the sky didn't help. These things had likely nested in his subconscious mind like the disease they were and now he was experiencing the fallout from it.

The wind slammed the carpet of snow covering the ground, causing it to heave and drift as wet flakes spattered and stuck to the window.

The house was outfitted with old-fashioned functional shutters, and he considered venturing outside to close and latch them. They'd better protect the windows, particularly once the wind grew increasingly violent and began snapping branches and whatnot. But they'd also completely seal him off from the outside world. He'd no longer be able to see out unless he opened the front or back door.

And if you can't see out you won't know what's coming…

He nodded, though he still had no idea why he was having such thoughts in the first place, much less agreeing with them. Maybe it was more than the locals and their superstitious bullshit. Maybe it was simply clinical paranoia rearing its ugly head. After everything that had happened, didn't it stand to reason these kinds of feelings would manifest sooner or later? His life had been wiped away like a stain that no longer existed. Things and people he thought would always be there were gone and gone for good. Would he, *could* he ever truly feel secure again? After all, his whole world had been torn from him. "No," he muttered. "I gave it away."

I know you want to, Mr. B. It's OK. I do too.

And just like that Emma was back in his head, smiling that crooked smile and staring at him with her mischievous ice-blue eyes. He'd promised himself he would never again allow her to invade his thoughts, but then, what was one more broken promise?

Teardrops on an ocean…a match on a raging inferno…

Lane wanted to hate her, but thinking of Emma only made him despise himself even more than he already did. *What a fool I was,* he thought. *What a goddamn fool.* Some days it still didn't seem real. Even though he'd paid a very real price (and would likely continue to for the remainder of his life), a small part of him kept hoping it was all some cosmic error or a bad dream he hadn't yet awakened from. He'd replay the events over and over again in his mind and still struggled to understand how he'd allowed such a thing to happen. He focused again on the snowstorm. His truck was already caked with a fine coating of white, and the flakes were beginning to spatter and stick to the window, obscuring his view.

How long's it been since somebody put their arms around you?

Marla's memory came as a distraction, though not a pleasant one. Clyde Reeve had told him about Snead's wife weeks before in passing, but he never suspected he'd actually go see her. In fact at the time he'd laughed it off, claiming he had no interest in prostitutes when Clyde gave him the address and said, "We all got needs, figured maybe you could use some company. Ashamed to say I go myself now and then. She's not so bad, really." Now not only had he gone through with it, he'd behaved like some pathetic fool, sitting on the bed next to her, holding her and crying like a child while she stroked his forehead and whispered everything would be all right. Even afterward, when his time had run out and she told him it was either time to go or pay for another thirty minutes, she seemed genuinely saddened for him. Imagine. *She* felt sorry for *him*. A woman pimped by her husband, who spent her days smoking meth and having sex with locals and strangers for money while their young daughter played just feet away.

Lane was just about to turn from the window when a battered full-size pickup he recognized as Clyde's came into view, pulled onto the property and slid in next to his truck. He hadn't been expecting him but wasn't surprised. With such a bad storm on the way it was just like Clyde to stop by, see if he needed anything and make sure Lane was properly prepared.

Clyde Reeve was a tall and lanky man in his early fifties. With angular features, a thick salt-and-pepper mustache and a mane of shoulder-length silver hair, he had the look of an aging cowboy or a 70s porn star. Lane first met him through the real estate agent that sold him the house. The property was in need of basic repairs and the agent recommended Clyde as a reliable jack-of-all-trades who did good work quickly and affordably. They'd hit it off immediately, mostly because unlike near everyone else in Edgar, Clyde was not a native. Although he was accepted in the community as one of their own, he didn't share the same guarded attitude toward outsiders. He'd lived there for years but had been born and raised in Oklahoma. He'd joined the Marines in his youth, and upon his discharge had married a woman originally from Edgar, settled there and raised two kids. Five years ago, he'd lost his wife to cancer. His children were grown and had both moved away a few years prior. Maybe it was their shared sense of loneliness, of loss, that had brought them together. Regardless, since moving to town, Clyde was the only person he considered even close to a friend.

"Uncle Clyde's here," he told Vince. The dog looked at him, wagged his tail then resumed mauling his chew toy.

He watched as Clyde hopped down out of his truck and sauntered across the yard to the front door, stopping twice to look up at the sky, eyes squinting against the onslaught of snowflakes. He had something bulky under his arm Lane couldn't identify, and in his other hand was a small beef bone.

Lane opened the door. "Didn't expect to see you out in this mess."

"Nothing much to it yet." Clyde stepped into the mudroom, closed the door behind him and held out a pair of wooden snowshoes. "Brought these over for you, figured you probably didn't have a pair of your own."

"Snowshoes? Seriously?"

"Hey, these storms up here are no joke."

"I know, but *snowshoes*?"

Clyde brushed his snow-damp hair back and away from his face. "Trust me, if we get what they think's coming you'll need these to get around. Don't suppose you've ever used them before."

"Nope, can't say as I have."

"Want to strap them on and take a quick trial run?"

"If I end up needing them I can figure it out. Not that complicated, right?"

"You'd be surprised."

Lane accepted the shoes and set them down in the corner. "Thanks for thinking of me, I appreciate it. Come on in, have a seat and warm up."

He held up the small bone. "Where's my boy?"

"Doing unspeakable things to that poor duck of his."

Vince was still preoccupied with the chew toy but the moment Clyde stepped into the kitchen the dog saw him and charged, hopping and barking and licking him as if he hadn't seen him in months.

Dropping into a crouch, Clyde petted and played with the dog then handed over the bone. The puppy snatched it, ran to the corner and curled up with it.

"Anybody ever breaks in, the best I can hope for is he licks them to death." Lane motioned to the coffee pot on the counter. "Cup of coffee?"

"Sure wouldn't turn one down." Clyde rose to his feet, removed his coat and slung it over the back of a kitchen chair. "Damnedest thing, Lane."

"What's that?" From the moment Clyde had arrived Lane

knew there was something bothering him. He had an unusually dark and concerned expression, and Lane had also caught a whiff of alcohol on his breath. Like Lane, he was a bit of a drinker, but not this early in the day. "Everything all right?"

"Dwight Maynard," he said sullenly, and then realizing Lane wasn't sure who that was added, "fella owns the farm, sells blueberries."

"Oh yeah, right." Lane knew of him, but didn't know the man personally.

"His wife found him dead this morning."

"Oh, I'm sorry. Were you good friends?"

"Known him for years. Dwight was good people."

"He didn't look that old." Lane filled the coffee pot then poured it into the Mr. Coffee and switched it on. "What, early sixties maybe?"

"Yeah, sixty-four."

"What a shame, that's too young." He pulled two mugs down from the cupboard as the coffeemaker gurgled to life. "What happened?"

"That's the thing, nobody's sure, least not yet anyway. Like there wasn't already enough crazy shit going on in town these days. The Staties are there now with an ambulance and some other mucky-mucks trying to figure things out. Tell you one thing, this snow ain't helping. Jenny—that's Dwight's wife—she called a few of us this morning to let us know so we went over to see if there was anything we could do. Cops were still about half an hour or so out. I got over there right around the time the other fellas did. Pretty sure Jenny was in shock. Too calm, you know? She was in a haze, like a robot or something, no emotion at all. Said their dog Blue woke them up late last night making a fuss so Dwight got up and took him out. She didn't think anything of it, rolled over and went back to sleep. This morning she woke up and Dwight wasn't in bed. She goes downstairs and he's nowhere to be found. But the dog's crying and clawing at the back door. Poor thing's paws were bleeding and he was scared to death. He'd taken damn near two inches off the bottom of that door. I figured Blue must've been scratching at it trying to get in for hours. But he never barked. Jenny said if he'd barked she would've heard him. So the three of us—me, Jed Hutch and Curly Briggs—all followed Jenny out to the back of the property. Blue wouldn't budge. I've never seen an animal that scared in all my life. When we got out there, I started to understand why." He stretched his long legs out across the floor, his boots dripping water as he did so. "Do me a favor. Throw a little something extra in that coffee, would you?"

"Yeah. Sure." Lane found a bottle of whiskey in another cupboard, walked it over to the table and set it down. "You all right, Clyde?"

"Just a little shook up is all." He rubbed his eyes. "See, way at the back of the property there's this big hill. Other side there's nothing but forest. We get out there, and Dwight's laying right at the top of this hill, on his back, arms out at his sides, eyes wide open. Naked as a newborn, didn't have a stitch of clothing on. And his skin looked…Lane it looked *burned*. All red like a lobster, you know? In some parts it was so bad there was little blisters all around."

"Christ."

"Damnedest goddamn thing I ever seen."

As the coffee finished brewing, Lane poured some into both mugs then joined Clyde at the table. "Maybe it was from the cold. You know, frostbite can often look like—"

"This wasn't frostbite. I know frostbite and this wasn't that." He snatched up the bottle and poured a healthy amount into his mug. "Picture a really bad chemical burn and you'll get an idea."

Lane nodded but wasn't sure what else to say.

"No other trauma or marks on him we could see, but didn't nobody want to touch him or disturb the crime scene. You know, like they always say you ought not to on those CSI shows on TV."

"Do you think there was foul play involved?"

"Something *foul* about the whole goddamn thing."

"Anything that pointed to murder though?"

Using both hands, Clyde gripped the mug, slowly brought it to his mouth and took a long sip. "Not exactly, but here's the thing. Jenny said when Dwight left the house he was wearing pajamas and a robe. His boots weren't in the front hall where he always left them so she figures he slipped them on too. But none of his clothes were anywhere around."

"Strange."

"Gets stranger. Besides Jenny's there weren't any footprints out there. Not one. It'd been snowing, and there was already snow on the ground from the dusting a few days ago. There wasn't enough accumulation of the fresh snow yet to cover tracks, even if they were made in the middle of the night, but she said there weren't any footprints leading to the hill or going up the hill when she found him. How the hell could Dwight get up there without leaving footprints behind? And believe me when I tell you, I saw for myself, but for Jenny's there were no footprints going up or down that hill and none around the base of it. Not one. Hell, Jenny's prints only went about halfway up. She told me once she saw Dwight's body there she knew he was dead so she turned and ran for the house. But you see what I'm saying here? It's not possible for him to get to the top of that hill without leaving tracks." He drank from the mug again. "Noticed something else too. The snow cover was pristine so it was easy to see that Dwight's body was sunk down a ways in the snow. Almost like—I know this sounds crazy but—almost like he'd been *dropped* there."

Lane sipped his coffee. "Dropped."

"From above. Like from a helicopter or something maybe."

"A helicopter?"

"Or something."

Lane watched him a moment then laughed lightly, nervously. "Oh come on, not more of this UFO and little green men nonsense."

"From everything I've ever read, they're not green." His face didn't even hint at a smile. "I don't know if you know this, but Dwight's one of the people in town that reported seeing them lights in the sky. Couple days back I ran into him and asked him about it. He said they were out over his property at night a bunch of times, once for almost half an hour. Said he'd never seen anything like them."

"I bet not, but they could've been any number of—"

"Said he was having bad dreams too, nightmares that didn't make sense, said they were making him paranoid."

Clyde's words caught him like a slap to the face but he did his best to appear unaffected. "That's rough, I mean—it must've been terrible for him, I—"

"Hell, I don't know if I believe in all that UFO crap either, but it goes all the way back to even before the Bible, you know. Some people believe the little bastards have been coming here for thousands of years. Been recorded by every culture all over the planet throughout human history, including the oldest ever, the Sumerians, so who's to know for sure? Lot of different theories out there—everything from spacemen to inter-dimensional beings to fallen angels—some even think they're us, visiting from the future. I always liked that one."

Unsure of how to respond, Lane said nothing.

"Government knows all about it. People like to roll their eyes and act like only nuts and fools believe in these things, but I'm telling you, there's something to it. What exactly, I don't know, but it's not nothing."

"OK, so what about Dwight?"

Clyde shrugged. "Don't know for sure what happened, only know it don't make any sense."

Lane tried to shift gears. "Does anyone around here own a helicopter?"

"Company down in Portland leases them, but the only time you see one in these parts is during picking season. Cranberry growers hire them. During dry harvest, the growers dump the berries into these big bins. To save wear and tear on the bogs they use helicopters to lift the bins and put them down off to the side or on trailers and whatnot. Picking season ended a couple weeks ago, though, runs late September to early November in these parts. Either way, what the hell would Dwight be doing in a helicopter, especially in the middle of the night? And what's more, if a copter was that close to the house Jenny would've heard it. Ever been near one? They ain't exactly quiet, make one hell of a racket." He ran a hand through his hair. "Just the same, *something* dropped him there. Unless Dwight learned how to fly there's no other explanation I know of."

The whole thing sounded ludicrous, but Lane nodded kindly anyway. Clyde was a salt-of-the-earth, no-nonsense type of individual who didn't spook easily or seem susceptible to flights of fantasy. If what he'd said about the lack of footprints was true—and Lane had no reason to believe it wasn't—they were dealing with one hell of a mystery. "Were there any tracks from Dwight at all?"

"Just leading from the front door out into the yard. They stopped about halfway across the property, same as the dog's did. Then there were tracks showing Blue turning tail and running back for the house."

Despite the heat in the room, Lane shivered.

"And what the hell could've burned Dwight like that?" Clyde asked.

Lane considered the possibilities a moment. "Radiation maybe?"

"Could be. Don't know much about that."

"Could it have been a suicide? If he took all his clothes off and laid down he had to know he'd freeze to death."

"Dwight ain't the type, but even if he did get undressed and lay down, where are his clothes and where are the tracks? *How did he get up there?*"

"Did the cops have any theories?"

"Staties were tight-lipped as ever." He reached for the bottle again and added another splash of whiskey to his coffee. "Thing is them and the EMTs were only there a few minutes before these other fellas showed up. Suits. Looked like feds, all official and serious. One of them told me to stay put, that they wanted to talk to me. By this time me and the other guys and even Jenny were back at the house, the cops got us out of there right quick, let me tell you. After a few minutes the suits come back from the hill and start asking for names and addresses and questioning us about what happened and what we saw."

"What'd you do?"

"Told the truth. They wrote down what we said and went back out to where Dwight was. Then one of the Staties came around, said we could leave."

"Did these suits identify themselves?"

"The one that questioned me said he was a federal agent."

"What, like FBI?"

"Not sure, never saw any ID."

"Did you ask for some?"

"I figured he'd show me a badge or something but he never did." Clyde stroked his mustache. "So I asked him why federal agents would be there and he said it was just procedure. When I told him plenty of people had passed in this town over the years but I never once saw the government show up to check it out, he said that was none of my concern. Pissed me off but I let it go because to be honest the guy gave me the creeps. Strange eyes. Dead eyes, like a doll, you know? Like there was nothing there once you got past them. So I answered his questions and got the hell out of there."

"Were they driving any kind of official vehicle?"

"Big black SUVs. No markings on them. Government plates."

Lane thought a moment. "Was Dwight involved in anything he shouldn't have been, or did he have any kind of past maybe no one knew about?"

"A simple man, a good man, that's all Dwight Maynard was. Why the hell would the feds give a damn about some dead blueberry farmer in Edgar? And tell me this. The state cops got there about thirty minutes after Jenny called them. That's normal unless they already happen to be in the area, which is rare. But they were only on the scene maybe ten minutes when the federal guys showed up. If the Staties called them, how the hell did they get there so fast? There aren't any FBI offices anywhere near this part of the state."

"Seems to me if they were FBI agents they'd identify themselves as such."

"Well whatever the hell they were they got here awful fast."

"Maybe they were nearby working on something else and when the state cops requested federal involvement they got the call."

Clyde thought about it a moment. "Could be. Least that makes sense."

"You're right though, that is one strange scenario all the way around."

"Awful lot of *strange scenarios* in this town lately. Too many, you ask me. Something's not right with any of it. I can feel it."

Vince suddenly chomped on his chew toy and it squeaked, startling both men. Clyde forced a smile and absently scratched at the stubble on his chin. "Well, time will tell, I guess."

"I'm sorry about Dwight, hope they get to the bottom of it. Kind of creepy."

"That it is." Clyde sat forward and gave the table a slap, indicating it was time for a new topic. "So, wanted to make sure you were all set. You got more than enough wood to get you through a few days. I'd suggest getting some gas into the generator and moving it up here into the mudroom before things get too messy out there. Might not end up needing it but if you do you sure as hell don't want to be wheeling that sumbitch through two feet of snow."

"Sounds like a plan. I appreciate you looking out for me, Clyde."

"You just stay hunkered down and you'll be fine. Soon as I can I'll be over to plow you out." He took another pull of coffee then stood up and stretched a bit. "Now let's go see about that generator and get you battened down, I told the guys I'd head out for a while with them, maybe get a little hunting in."

"In this storm?"

"Aw hell," Clyde chuckled, "this ain't a storm. Not yet."

At this point in Boston the grocery stores would've been packed with frantic shoppers, schools would've closed and people would've been hurrying home. Up here, it evidently had to get far worse before people paid attention.

"Won't be a storm for a few hours yet," he added. "Figured after that business over at Dwight's it'd do us good to head out a while. You ought to come with us one of these days."

"Hunting's not my thing." Lane had purchased a shotgun not long after he moved to Edgar but had yet to fire it. In fact, he hadn't fired a gun of any kind in years. "I couldn't kill unless it was in self-defense."

"Only thing we ever kill is time. It's mostly an excuse to get out and away from everything a spell, walk around out in the woods, have a little peace."

A while later, after they'd readied the generator, gotten it up to the house and Clyde had headed home, Lane took

Vince for a lengthy walk around the property. The snow was slowly building, gradually getting worse, and he knew the opportunities to take the dog out to do his business would progressively become fewer and farther between. He couldn't shake the story Clyde had told him, and kept trying to figure out how Dwight Maynard could've gotten to the summit of that hill without leaving tracks. He knew Clyde well enough to be certain he'd never lie about such things. Yet it simply wasn't possible. Either Clyde was mistaken, or as he suggested, Dwight had been dropped there from above. Lane couldn't help but wonder if any of this had to do with his recent feelings of paranoia and being watched. Maybe something truly unexplainable *was* happening in this town and he had somehow sensed or tapped into it.

Christ, I sound like a lunatic.

The snow whipped about, stinging his cheeks and scratching at his eyes. Lane gave Vince's leash a gentle tug. The dog had finished relieving himself and had spent the last few minutes frolicking about and enjoying the snowfall. Lane looked up. The sky was mostly obscured with blowing snow, but he could make out the trees along the back of the property just beyond the outbuilding. Their branches, curled, twisted and dark, stripped bare as blackened bones, shifted in the wind, reaching for him through the whirlwind of flakes. He pictured something moving rapidly through the trees, closing on him like a violently charging animal disguised as a rush of wind and bringing with it darkness and feelings of dread and hatred Lane couldn't even begin to fully comprehend.

Something brushed his leg.

Vince had moved closer and was sitting at Lane's feet, his playful and carefree manner replaced with something more sullen and distracted. Watching the same trees, his little dark eyes squinted and blinked rapidly.

"You feel it too," Lane mumbled. "Don't you?"

The dog moved closer still, pushing his way between Lane's feet until he was sitting between his legs.

Almost like he's trying to hide.

Lane wiped snow from his eyes and continued staring at

the trees, but they offered nothing more. A quiet filled the air, the kind one experiences only in winter. It is an eternal and final sound of silence one feels down to the deepest recesses of one's being. But on this day, there was something within that silence Lane had never experienced before.

He couldn't hear them, but he knew what they were. He could feel them so strongly they might as well have been emanating from his own throat. Screams. Bloodcurdling screams of horror, pain and unimaginable terror. Yet they didn't make a sound.

There was only the wind.

Clutching the leash tightly, Lane turned and led Vince back to the house.

THREE

There is something about this particular blackbird in the window that concerns him. There is something…wrong…something wrong with this blackbird.

"Who are you?" he asks it.

The barking gets louder…closer… and the familiar click of his dog's nails on the floor distracts him, tears him from the eyes of the blackbird.

There, in the doorway to his bedroom, is the dog, barking and wagging his tail with equal ferocity. Same as the dog, he isn't sure if he should be happy or frightened. Strange. Why should he be frightened of his own puppy?

It is then he realizes the dog is no longer the puppy he once was. Though not yet a full grown dog, he is considerably larger than he was previously. But how could that be?

Time. It's not right. It's backward, it's…wrong…blurred somehow…

He remembers a bit more. How long ago was it that these horrible wounds were inflicted upon him?

Days? Weeks? Months?

The dog is virtually unharmed. He remembers wrapping him in the only blanket he had, keeping the puppy warm rather than himself.

"It's OK, boy," he tells the dog, his voice unfamiliar and slurred.

The dog backs away into the other room. The barking ceases.

He wonders if he's dreaming. Yes, I…I must be.

After all, that horrible night was in the past. He survived it. Imprisoned by what he could never tell anyone, he'd fallen from the darkness just as the Lords of Twilight had fallen from the heavens, through the night to the blinding light of winter.

The authorities found him in the snow, in the aftermath of an epic winter storm, collapsed and dying, his faithful pup at his side and refusing to leave him even when they transported him to the hospital via ambulance. "They're here," he managed to tell those working so furiously to save him. But they could not hear him.

No one could.

Still, this makes no sense. That was all in the past. It's over with now and he's safe, he has returned to Boston and lives with his friend Russell. He has plans to put his life back together and begin again. So how could—

From the corner of his eye he sees movement and follows it to the window. The blackbird is still there, still staring at him with those horrible black eyes. What does it want? Those eyes, they…they're so…it's like they can see right through him and yet there is something undeniably mesmerizing about them. Fearful they're hypnotizing him somehow, he tries to look away but can't. So he studies them harder, staring into the inky pools and allowing them to take him deeper until he sees his own dark reflection in them.

And behind him, something else…someone standing in the corner of the bedroom…

The house filled with the smell of homemade beef stew. Lane had made and refrigerated a batch the day before and returned a portion of it to the top of the woodstove to heat it up. He dipped a wooden spoon into the mixture—chunks of beef, carrots, potatoes, onion and celery—and gave it a healthy stir. The thick gravy bubbled and popped, so he removed it from the heat and placed the pan on the counter. Vince's tail slapped Lane's leg, signaling he'd followed him from the den to the kitchen. "Smells pretty good, doesn't it?" The tail wagged faster. "Sorry pal, you're still too little for people food." To illustrate his disagreement, Vince gave a grumbling moan somewhere between a low growl and a whine, so Lane grabbed a dog treat from a plastic bag on the counter he'd been using to aid in training and handed one over. Vince took it but was less than enthused with the payoff. As Lane tore a hearty piece of Italian bread from a fresh loaf and fixed himself a bowl of stew, Vince stayed close, hoping for a spill or renegade crumb. When Lane sat at the table and began to eat, the dog realized it wasn't to be, and with a defeated sigh, curled up at his feet.

Unfortunately, even the simple pleasure of a tasty meal was short-lived.

As Lane chased some stew with a sip of beer his mind wandered and he found himself thinking about his ex-wife Claire. It was her recipe, after all, she'd taught him how to make it. It was impossible to move through even his mundane existence without thinking of her regularly. Everywhere he looked, she was there. With the exception of his childhood, she haunted each and every memory as either a main character or a peripheral extra. And why shouldn't she? Claire had been the love of his life, and he'd been hers. He wondered what she was doing at that exact moment. He hadn't seen her in more than a year. Did she look the same? Did she ever think of him? Did she miss him? Did she miss *them* as much as he did? Had she moved on and started dating yet? Would he ever have a chance to just sit and talk with her again? How extraordinary the simple things he'd once taken for granted seemed now. He'd have given just about anything to sit and watch television with her the way they'd once done, or spend an afternoon curled up on the couch reading or going out to dinner together to one of their favorite restaurants. He'd lost his wife, best friend and confidant all in the single stroke of a pen, and a life where he didn't have to consider Claire because she no longer played a part in it was still foreign to him. Worse, it not only made for a hopelessly lonely existence, but one he felt the need to question constantly. Was it necessary, this so-called life he was leading? Was *he* necessary? The two things that most defined him—being a husband and his career as a teacher—were no longer a part of his life, so what the hell was the point?

He picked at the stew, his appetite gone.

In the couple hours since Clyde had left, the storm had picked up quite a bit. The wind was steadily becoming stronger, coming in increasingly violent bursts that shook and rattled the small house and blew the snow into mounting drifts. He imagined Clyde and the others stumbling through the forest with their hunting rifles, looking for deer and aliens, soundless helicopters, flying saucers and MIB hiding in the trees. Madness. Lane slid the bowl of stew away, stood up and strode into the bathroom just off the kitchen. In a small mirror over the sink, his reflection froze him in his tracks. He barely recognized himself. The younger, healthier and better-looking version he saw in his mind and memory had virtually no relation to the man staring back at him. The lines in his face had deepened considerably in the last year, his complexion had grown pale and haggard, and his thinning hair had turned almost entirely gray. His eyes were glassy, dim, saddled with black bags and locked in a perpetual state of sorrow. He looked exhausted. Ravaged. Ruined.

Lane grabbed his beer and retreated to the den, Vince following dutifully on his heels. It was a cramped and dim little room, with its low ceilings and cheap yard sale furniture. The two windows facing the front of the property were caked with snow, making visibility beyond them difficult. He stood there a moment and watched the storm. Snow and rain dripped along the pane, trickled down the casing. One piece of ice in particular caught Lane's eye, and he watched it slide along the glass until it fell from sight.

Looking back on it later, he assured himself it had only been a trick of the light or the fault of his tired, bleary eyes. But in the moment, he saw something that defied the laws of physics. The window rippled, moving like a sheet of water might, in liquid motion from the bottom of the pane to the top, as if for just a second the solid piece of glass had transformed into a slowly coursing wave gently rolling across the surface of the window. And in that strange and disconcerting moment, the storm beyond the window ceased to exist, replaced instead with darkness the depths and totality of which Lane had never before seen or even imagined. An endless night void of life or warmth, barren and unforgiving… silent and still…

Like space, he thought, *a vast expanse of cold, empty space.*

Lane glanced down at the beer bottle in his grasp. His hand was shaking. The window, and everything beyond it, had returned to normal. This time the dog seemed unaffected.

The window had apparently been Lane's hallucination and Lane's alone. He rubbed his eyes with his free hand.

"Hell's happening to me?"

With a sigh he moved to a comfortable chair in the corner and sat down. On the small table next to it was a remote control and the book he'd been reading, a dog-eared edition of Somerset Maugham's novel *The Painted Veil*. He'd first read it in college, and as many of his books were among the few material possessions he'd left the marriage with, he'd decided to spend much of his newfound free time rereading some of the works he'd enjoyed in his youth. This novel in particular, with its themes of betrayal and a damaged marriage, had been tough going due to the subject matter, which concerned a husband, who upon discovering his wife's infidelities, insists she accompany him from their native England to Hong Kong, and into the midst of a cholera epidemic, costing her the life, standing and spoiled safety she had previously attained and taken for granted, but also eventually revealing to both she and her husband the true meaning of love, life, loss, personal sacrifice and the beauty of forgiveness, not only of others, but of oneself.

Lane grabbed the remote control and activated a modest tabletop stereo system located on a low stand beneath the windows. Yo-Yo Ma's melancholy and deeply moving CD *Appassionato* came to life, filling the room with a sad and quiet beauty. He reached down, lifted Vince onto his lap and gave him a kiss on his cold, wet nose. "Who's my little man?" The puppy responded with a loving gaze then lay down, rested his chin on Lane's knee and promptly fell asleep. Turning his attention to the novel, Lane flipped to his bookmark and did his best to lose himself in Maugham's wonderful prose.

Beyond the walls of his delicate cocoon, the storm raged on.

Water. Dripping. He assumed at first that it must have been the snow melting and running from the drains outside, trickling from the trees and gushing along the dirt driveway. But no, it was…closer. Inside, they… these water sounds were coming from inside the house, from inside the…house? No…not the house… because he wasn't in the house. Not anymore.

He was somewhere else now…

It wasn't until he opened his eyes that he realized he'd been plunged into darkness. Total. Encompassing. Hopeless.

There was an odd taste in his mouth, a metallic flavor that coated his gums and tongue and made him sick to his stomach. Each time he swallowed it got worse, and when he tried to reach up and put his fingers to his lips, he was just barely able to move. Trapped, he…

Where the hell am I?

He attempted to kick his feet, and although he could move his legs, his range of motion was so limited he couldn't even fully bend his knees. He tried to sit up but something held him in place, something malleable but strong that stretched like a hideous skin encasing his entire body.

Realizing he'd been wrapped in some sort of foreign material, he panicked and began to struggle and cry out for help. The membrane stretched and moved with him but refused to break no matter how hard he struggled, and his cries were muffled and weak, as if someone had placed a hand over his mouth.

As his body surrendered to its pliable prison, Lane sensed motion. Similar to the sinking feeling in one's gut one experiences as an elevator comes to a stop, it rippled up through his bowels and into his chest in a single wave of nausea then receded as quickly as it arrived.

Whispers…odd clicking noises in recurring patterns reminiscent of language…the sound of motion, a whooshing sound of fabric dragging across a floor perhaps, but…but those whispers, they—they wouldn't stop, soft and echoing as if spoken from the far end of a long and desolate tunnel. Although he could not recognize them as words, he was certain they were not gibberish either. There was purpose, urgency, but they were wrong. All wrong.

They weren't human.

And then, Emma, standing so close—too close—and smelling like candy, bathed in some icky-sweet scent designed, packaged and marketed to appeal to young teens. Who else would want to smell like a cherry bubblegum lozenge? What was she doing here? Why…

"Hey Mr. B.," she said with a coy smile, widening her eyes and resting the tip of her thumb on her bottom lip. "What's up?" Had someone taught her this? Did she see it in a movie or on television? These kids today, they weren't like Lane was at that age. They weren't even children anymore, not really, and not for long. Nor were they adults, but instead a sad and disturbing hybrid of myths and false, media-driven depictions and expectations. They were fabrications dictated by Madison Avenue, characters based on people who never truly existed. Emma was fourteen-years-old and already dressed, behaved and spoke like she believed a much older woman might. But her portrayal was skewed, silly, misguided and horribly uninformed. Two or three years ago she was playing with toys. Now she had a crush on a teacher old enough to be her father and tried to seduce him by sending suggestive indications she might begin sucking her thumb at any moment. "Mr. B.? I said, what's up?"

He tried to speak but it came out garbled. Somehow he could see her through the skin-like wrap but remained blind to everything else. As if seeing her as reflection…but where—or what—was the mirror? That outfit, who—who would let their teenage daughter out of the house looking like that? What was wrong with her parents?

I've been doing this a long time, kid, and I've seen it all before, trust me. Schoolgirl crushes happen all the time, no big deal, they're easy to disarm and control. They have to be nipped in the bud and dealt with kindly but firmly, that's the key. You're the student and I'm the teacher. You're a kid and I'm an adult. The lines between appropriate and inappropriate behavior are very clear if one chooses to see them. I am a happily married man with neither the desire nor the inclination to become involved with a teenage girl. And you're confusing infatuation, transference and maybe even some genuine lust for love and true affection. I'm sorry your father didn't give you enough of his time and attention, but I'm not him and I can't be a substitute. Stop trying to make me your boyfriend. It's your father you're looking for, Emma, not me, not some other man, not even the boys in school who so eagerly follow you around hoping for a chance to get under your shirt and into your pants. Stop trying to give people what you think they want. It won't make them love you, Emma. It won't heal those wounds, that void your father hasn't filled. Stop trying to be what you think a grownup is because you're failing miserably and only embarrassing yourself. Be a kid. Enjoy that while you still can because before you know it—

Movement...something moving behind her...near her... near him... but it was so strange...like the whole world was shifting, moving along with her, the entire scene swallowed into a curiously shaped black mirror.

No. Two black mirrors.

The strange clicking noises were back. They sounded almost like insects, like shelled bugs scuttling about and...

That wasn't Emma. You tricked me, you—how did you get in my head? Get out, I—I don't want you in my head, it hurts, it—you're hurting me—stop, don't, I—I won't open my eyes. I promise I won't open my eyes. I don't want to see, I—I'm afraid to see. I'm afraid so—so afraid so—oh please, the dark it's—it's so dark but...

The darkness took form. There was substance to it. So close but moving slowly away, it took shape.

Oh God...My God...help me.

Sharp, high-pitched barks rang through the room and suddenly Lane was standing, staggering from the chair and stumbling about the room. The novel in his lap fell to the floor as Vince, who had at some previous point retreated to the kitchen doorway, cowered and continued to bark at him. *Did I fall asleep?*

Lane crouched down to reassure the dog. His throat was sore. Had he been screaming? Is that what had frightened the puppy so? "Come on, it's OK."

Vince, still cowering but no longer barking, began to slowly slink closer. Eventually he sniffed at Lane's hand and allowed him to pet him. "It's me, buddy, it's me." Lane scooped the puppy up in his arms, kissed his nose and carried him over to the windows, heart racing. "I must've fallen asleep and had a bad dream, I..." his eyes began to adjust and it was then that he realized it was darker in the den than when he'd first sat down to read. It was still light out but night was coming fast and the storm had gotten much worse.

As he glanced at his watch, his eyes narrowed in disbelief. He hadn't nodded off for a moment or two as he'd originally suspected.

It was nearly four-thirty. The entire afternoon was gone.

He'd been asleep for more than three hours.

FOUR

He spins, looks behind him. Someone dressed entirely in black stands facing the corner, back to him. Everything about this person is black, the hair, the skin, everything. But it's not…normal. It's almost as if the blackbird has somehow transformed itself into a form decidedly more human.

He laughs a little because that's not possible but…but there's nothing funny about it. No. No…there's nothing funny about any of this.

They've come back for him.

Who is that? Who is in his room, standing there and facing the corner like a punished child?

"Child," he says softly.

Yes, that's it. It looks almost like a child. Small…short…

But this is no child. This is something else.

I don't want you to turn around. Don't turn around—I don't want to see—

Screams. Horrifying, piercing screams emanating from someone so frightened that all control has been lost to abject, mindless, uncontrollable terror.

As he turns back to the window, he realizes the screams are his own.

Unmoved, the blackbird watches him with its dead eyes.

And then he realizes something else, something far more sinister.

That's not a blackbird. In fact, it's not a bird at all.

Behind him, that which he does not want to see—not ever again—not ever, don't—please dear God don't ever make me see it again—shuffles closer…

And as the blackbird that is not a blackbird reaches for him, its long spidery fingers crawling impossibly closer through the glass, something grabs hold of him from behind and snatches him with violent and sudden force, his body awkwardly catapulting backward as if yanked away by unseen hands.

In the mudroom, Vince did the happy dance as Lane poured some dry food into his bowl. The dog pounced and began devouring the kibble as if he hadn't eaten in ages.

Lane tossed the scoop back into the bin and snapped the lid down tight. "Easy, buddy, no one's going to take it from you."

While the puppy crunched away Lane noticed that just beyond the window several inches had accumulated on the front porch and blown in a growing drift against the door. While he realized he'd likely have to repeat this several times, if he didn't clear some snow out now, by the time the blizzard was over he'd never get the storm door open. Determined to stay ahead of it, he grabbed a shovel from the closet and slipped on his coat. As he pulled his knit hat down over his ears, the entire house began to tremble. Dishes in the cupboards clinked against each other and unseen things rattled and shook as a low rumble that at first sounded like distant thunder grew steadily louder.

A flash of light on the road burned through the whiteout just as a large vehicle rolled into view. Several more followed, their yellow emergency lights spinning ominously and slashing at the curtains of snow. Initially Lane assumed they were plows, but their markings suggested military vehicles of some kind, and pulling up the rear were two enormous black SUVs. As the convoy vanished into the storm the house settled and the menacing rumble faded. Lane had counted ten vehicles in all.

Snow spattered against the lone mudroom window, the wind groaned like a wounded animal, and Lane stood there a while, holding his shovel and trying to convince himself it was a mere coincidence that the convoy had headed in the direction of Dwight Maynard's farm.

Lane shoveled a wide area out around the front door and cleared off the porch steps as best he could, but the snow was coming so fast now and with such ferocity that it was essentially pointless. Any evidence he'd shoveled at all would more than likely be lost within an hour or so. Out of breath, he stood at the base of the porch steps, leaned on his shovel and watched the road a while. No more vehicles of any kind.

No signs of life at all.

He wondered if at that very moment there was even one other human being on the planet thinking of him. If he ceased to exist or was suddenly swallowed up and carried away by the storm, would anyone notice? He supposed Clyde would when he eventually came to plow him out, but beyond that, would anyone truly care? Russell would mourn him, and surely Claire would feel badly. Hopefully some of the students he'd taught over the years might remember him fondly and be saddened to hear of his passing. But soon as those fleeting regrets faded, he'd become a distant memory, a footnote in time with no other proof or legacy to prove he'd ever existed at all. In all the years he'd spent teaching he'd had a handful of students thank him, usually those who had moved on through college and become successful. But they were few and far between. Until he'd had such vast amounts of time to think and reflect on his life, Lane had always assumed that had more to do with the students than it did him. But perhaps he hadn't been the teacher he thought he was. Maybe when it was all said and done he'd only reached those few kids, and had failed the rest.

I should've been a better teacher, he thought. *I could've been better, made more of an impact.* And therein lay the problem, because the same could be said of nearly every other avenue of his life as well. He could've been a better husband, a better friend and a better son. And that was just the start. The list was longer than he wanted to admit.

Then there was Claire. *God*, he thought, *how I miss her.*

It was the quiet things he missed most. The Sunday mornings snuggled up in bed, talking about everything and nothing at all, the walks after dinner and how even after all their years together they'd always hold hands, the laughter, the love, the safety, the trust. And all of it gone in a heartbeat, lost to memories and dreams. Who could've known life was so fragile?

He knew it was over; the divorce papers were final. There was no going back now. But he still felt the need to make things right with her. He owed her that much. If only he could get her to sit and listen to him for a minute, to talk with him a while and understand how much he loved and needed her. She knew those things were true, deep down she had to, and while what had happened had certainly been the catalyst for their breakup, the decision to either work things out or end it had ultimately rested with her. He knew she still loved him, or at least she had, but no longer wanted him. That much was clear. And although he couldn't blame her, he still struggled to understand how she'd been able to simply walk away from what had otherwise been a long and successful marriage.

They'd had something special once and had been deeply happy together for a very long time. Hadn't they?

He remembered her face the last day they discussed things, her eyes red and ringed with dark circles, face contorted with emotion, trembling hands fumbling with tissues and desperately wiping at her runny nose. She'd looked so impossibly frail that day, as if the slightest touch might shatter her to pieces. "Is it true?" she asked, voice cracking. "Lane, *is it true*?"

"No. It's not."

Her body bucked as she sobbed. "Yes it is." She brought the tissue to her eyes, dabbed them. "You're lying. I can tell."

"Nothing happened."

"You're lying."

"Nothing happened," he insisted. "And that's precisely why Emma's made these accusations. She's a scorned kid getting revenge, don't you see?"

"Then fight it."

"You heard what the lawyer said. If I do then this will be made public. There's likely to be a media frenzy where I'll be demonized, tried and convicted before we ever get anywhere near a courtroom, and even when we do it's her word against mine. In these cases the child is usually believed, even without any evidence and even when the teacher has no previous record or accusations of such behavior."

"Do you know why that is? Because the child is usually

telling the truth."

"For God's sake, why won't you believe me?"

"Because you're frightened."

"Of course I'm frightened. This girl has made accusations against me that could cost me everything. How am I supposed to feel?"

"It's the truth that scares you," Claire said evenly, a hint of disdain in her voice where before there had only been sorrow. "It always has."

"What's that supposed to mean?"

"You tell me."

"I'm in no mood for riddles, all right? Here's the reality of the situation. Even if I were to fight this and was found innocent of the charges, the publicity alone will ruin our lives. It'll ruin my career. We'll lose everything."

"We already have."

"It doesn't have to be this way. We can go somewhere else, start over."

"At our age? After all this?"

"What difference does it make as long as we still have each other?"

She lowered her gaze to the floor.

"Claire?" He stepped closer. "We *do* still have each other, don't we?"

He was still waiting for her answer.

A dark smudge moved along the edge of Lane's peripheral vision, snapping him back to the present. A large blackbird had landed on the porch and was sitting on the railing staring at him. He'd seen blackbirds in the yard many times before, but never one quite that size and never so close. He stood there a moment, his eyes locked on the bird's, and it seemed as if something passed between them, an understanding perhaps, unspoken and primal.

Neither moved for some time.

The sudden sound of branches breaking high up in the trees behind the house rang out through the storm. He spun in that direction but the house blocked his view of the forest behind it. It sounded like someone or something had fallen from one of the monstrous trees out back, snapping branches as it went.

When Lane looked back at the railing, the blackbird was gone.

Shovel in hand, he descended the steps then trudged his way around the side of the house until he had a clear view of the outbuilding and forest beyond. His eyes squinted through the blowing flakes, slowly scanning the forest for evidence of fallen branches. Nothing. Maybe it had happened deeper in the woods. Yes, he decided, that had to be it, because he'd definitely heard branches snapping. He pushed on, taking a few more steps into the deeper drifts along the side of the house, his breath escaping him in whirling clouds.

And then he saw them, and stopped where he was.

Unlike any he had ever seen before, pressed into the otherwise pristine snow covering the slanted roof of the outbuilding in a thick undisturbed layer, running up one side and disappearing over the summit…

Footprints.

Lane pawed snow from his face and eyes in a frantic attempt to make certain he was, in fact, looking at tracks of some kind. The snow was slowly covering them, absorbing them back into the white, but there was no mistaking the set of footprints on that roof. The first thought that came to mind was bird tracks, but these were far too big. Whatever had left them appeared to have three thick, long, distinct toes, and a very narrow heel, and their depth signaled whatever made them had far more weight behind it than any bird.

But no indigenous animal of that size left tracks even similar to that.

Gripping the shovel tight and holding it out before him as a weapon, Lane slid laterally through the snow, away from the house and toward the forest to his left, hoping for an angle where he could see the other side of the sloped roof without having to go behind the building. He'd nearly reached the trees when he saw that the tracks proceeded down the backside of the roof all the way to the edge. He craned his neck in an attempt to see the ground below, but there were no impressions there. If it hadn't dropped off the roof then it must've jumped into the trees. He looked to those closest to the backside of the roof.

They seemed undisturbed, but for occasionally rocking in the wind, their branches covered in snow and ice.

This is crazy, he thought. *They're bird tracks that became distorted in the storm. Of course that's it. They were made hours ago, maybe by that blackbird I saw on the porch, and as the wind and snow grew worse the tracks became altered, causing them to appear larger than they were when they'd been made.*

Suddenly something darted across a branch and dove from one tree to another.

Startled, Lane staggered back a few steps and nearly fell, only to realize it was just a squirrel. "Jesus H.," he said breathlessly, one hand still gripping the shovel, the other covering his pounding heart. A burst of laughter escaped him, equal parts nerves and relief. Watching the critter scurry along another branch before disappearing into the forest, Lane chuckled softly.

But then, emerging from the forest and headed in his direction, came a blur of movement, slow and methodical. A swath of shadow separating from the snow and growing darkness, it lumbered steadily closer through the trees.

And this was no squirrel.

Lane turned and ran for the house as best he could in the mounting snow, his eyes tearing, skin stinging in the cold and his mind racing in an attempt to logically explain his terror and what was happening. He'd nearly reached the porch when just above the cries of the wind he heard someone call his name.

Without slowing his stride, he looked back over his shoulder and saw that the shadow had cleared the trees and taken shape. It was three individuals running side-by-side rather than a single being. Three men, two holding up a third between them as they did their best to hurry through the storm.

Clyde Reeve and his two hunting buddies, Curly Briggs and Jed Hutch, struggling through the snow as fast as their legs would carry them. Clyde and Curly each had one of Jed's arms and were pulling him along. Both were clearly terrified and Jed looked only barely conscious, his head hung low and his legs dragging limply beneath him.

"Clyde?" Lane called out. "What's happening?"

"Get inside!" he screamed back. "You've got to get inside!"

Expecting them to join him and seek refuge in the house, Lane waited. But they remained where they were as if they'd encountered an invisible barrier they were unable to cross. Clyde handed Jed off to Curly and they staggered back into the woods from which they'd come, quickly swallowed by the snow.

"Where are they going, what—what's going on?"

"Get inside," Clyde said again, this time more evenly, his eyes heavy and sad. And like a vision from a fever dream, just before he turned and vanished into the snowy forest with the others, he gave a final woeful wave goodbye.

It was only then that Lane realized Clyde's hands were stained with blood.

Vince sat in the corner, unsure if he should be excited or concerned to see Lane frantically bounding into the house.

Once through the door, he made sure he closed it tight and locked it behind him, and as he stepped through the mudroom and into the kitchen, he saw the dog and said, "It's OK, buddy. Everything's OK."

His tail softly tapped the floor, but without its usual enthusiasm.

"Yeah, you're not buying it either, are you." He sighed, wiped his face free of ice and snow and leaned against the door. What the hell had just happened? Had he hallucinated or had Clyde and the others truly been there? If so, what was going on and why would they stop him simply to tell him to go back inside? And why wouldn't they join him in the house? Clearly Jed Hutch was badly injured and even Clyde had blood all over him. Had there been a hunting accident? None of it made a bit of sense.

Shaking, Lane led the puppy into the den then dropped onto the couch and tried to sort things out, but he was lost in a tangle of memories and nightmares, an ever-growing labyrinth he now feared he might never find his way out of. *Just calm down and think, goddamn it. Think.*

He reached down and petted Vince's head.

The shotgun you bought is in the bedroom closet. Get it. Load it.

Now.

With visions of the strange footprints and the three men still in his head, Lane made his way to the bedroom, retrieved the 12-gauge pump shotgun from the rear of the closet and then found the box of shells he'd purchased along with it in a drawer in the kitchen.

He sat in one of the kitchen chairs, and with trembling hands, loaded the shotgun. When he'd finished he put the box of shells aside on the table.

Lane noticed Vince sitting in the doorway, so he leaned the shotgun against the table then went over and picked him up. "It's OK, Vin, I'm right here."

The puppy was warm and plump.

He licked Lane's nose.

Despite the affection, fear rose from Lane's gut like bile bubbling up into the base of his throat. *You saw something you can't explain*, he told himself. *You were frightened and with all the unexplained occurrences in town lately you assumed it was something more than it really was, and so your mind filled in the blanks, giving you a vision of what you felt you should've seen but couldn't have. Not really, not truly.* But even as his brain tried desperately to find an explanation and a way out of this nightmare, he knew damn well he'd seen Clyde and the others. He'd heard Clyde call out and speak to him. He'd seen those footprints. Gently, Lane stroked Vince's head in the hopes that it might calm him and the puppy both, but his entire body had already begun to shake. His earlier dreams and visions coursed through his mind. The more he tried to suppress them the stronger they became. Lane held the puppy tight in the sparse light.

Off the kitchen, floorboards creaked in the bedroom… once…and again.

The dog's body tensed and a quiet whimper escaped him.

Someone else was in the house.

FIVE

In the silence of the house, the dog sits in the doorway and waits. For what, he cannot be sure. He only knows that eventually someone will come.

He can only hope it will not be more of them.

The screams are over now, but he can still hear them ringing in his ears like a bad dream. They make him shiver and cower even though he doesn't fully understand their origin. He only knows how they make him feel and how those who inspired them frighten him when they are near. In those frustrating times, when no one else knows, when he can smell and sense but not yet see them, he wants so desperately for the others to know, to warn them. And he tries, though it seldom seems to work. There is a shift in the air, a disturbance of balance in things that signals they're coming, and just as it registers, they've arrived and it's too late to do much of anything. Because by then they're standing right in front of him…behind him…all around him.

He longs for those vague and blurred days before this began, when he was new to this world himself and knew only happiness and joy, contentment and fulfillment.

Thoughts slink through his mind, and he focuses again on what has just taken place. He should've stopped it. But could he have?

No. Still…

The dog lays down in the doorway and sighs.

Bring him back. I don't know what to do without him.

The dog closes his eyes. He is aware of the markings Lane made on the walls in his own blood, but is unable to decipher meaning.

Finger-painted in manic, violent repetition is a single word. TAKEN.

Lane stood before the threshold to the bedroom, Vince at his side. The small room beyond was mostly dark, as the shades had been pulled down over the lone window. Shadows played along the walls and floor, shifting slightly.

Outside, in the sky overhead, a faint rumble grew louder and louder still as something large approached and flew over the house. Most likely a helicopter, it shook the entire house in the process, its thunderous grumbling so close it sounded as if it planned to land directly on the roof. Then as suddenly as it had arrived, the sound began to fade and soften until it had slipped away into the storm. In the quiet that followed, Lane forced a swallow and squinted to better see into the bedroom. He could've thrown the switch and illuminated the room, but something instinctually told him not to.

Wind and snow lashed the house.

Lane took a single tentative step over the threshold, moving into the room like he was stepping off the edge of a precipice and into the unknown. In a way that's exactly what he was doing, yet this time the fear had little effect on him. Rather than running, his trepidation actually drew him nearer. He glanced back over his shoulder. The dog remained on the other side of the open doorway, staring intently into the darkness but making no sound. Lane gave his leg a gentle slap, signaling Vince to follow him, but the puppy refused to obey. As he turned back toward the shadows and darkness of the bedroom, Lane smelled it. The unmistakable scent he'd known for so long. A chill throttled him. Remaining very still, he took in another breath and realized he hadn't been mistaken.

Hand shaking, he reached for the switch on the wall to his right. He didn't want to look, didn't want to see, but knew now he had no choice. There were not many things Lane could be sure of on this strange and cold night, but he had no doubt that someone was standing just beyond the far side of the bed, cradled in shadow. He still couldn't make out anything definitive, but he could smell them.

He could smell *her.*

Lane's hand hung in the darkness above the switch as he inhaled and again breathed in the cologne she had always worn. Faint, but unquestionably hers, he closed his eyes and waited. Nothing. Silence, eerie and pregnant. He opened his eyes, and without turning on the light after all, let his hand fall back to his side. He stepped closer. From shadows on the other side of the bed came the quiet, rhythmic sounds of someone breathing.

Frozen particles of snow ticked against the window, hidden by the shade.

Lane transferred his weight from one foot to the other, causing the light behind him from the kitchen to shift. He could now see that the figure by the bed was standing with her back to him. She looked like a rumor, a figment of his imagination there in the shadows, all angles and smudges and darkness and maybes and what-ifs. But it was definitely Claire, right there in front of him, not five feet away. Or something like her, attempting to be her, to trick him into believing it was his ex-wife.

She gazed back over her shoulder, not quite at him but near him, the whites of her eyes cutting the dark, blinking slowly, thoughtfully. As she had the last time he saw her, she looked horribly troubled, uncomfortable in her own skin, her own nightmares. Broken. She looked broken. Broken by him.

"Claire," he said, his voice so soft he barely heard it himself. It was not a question but not quite statement either, just a word tossed into the shadows moving between them, a stone thrown to oncoming waves, swallowed and gone so quickly it might have never existed in the first place.

Lane's heart raced and his chest tightened. It was only then that he realized he was pouring with sweat. Still, he couldn't take his eyes from her. Even though he knew there was no way she could really be standing there, he couldn't look away. *Am I asleep? Dreaming? Or have I truly lost my mind?*

"Who are you?" he asked, louder this time, voice shaking.

She faced him but remained largely concealed in shadow, her eyes staring straight into his now. "You know who I am."

"No," he said, "I don't."

Claire moved closer to the sparse light, revealing an outfit that included a tight tank-top T-shirt and a pair of jeans. She was barefoot and dressed more for summer, as if she'd just wandered in after a long walk on the beach, her dirty blonde hair a bit longer than he remembered it, parted in the middle and hanging in curls that cascaded down to her shoulders. As she so often did, she pulled her hair back and away from her face and combed it behind her ears with her fingers. Her wire rim eyeglasses were in place, troubled hazel eyes blinking behind the lenses. She'd always looked considerably younger than she really was, but time had begun to catch up to her even more than it had the last time he'd seen her. Claire, always a delicate cross between a quiet bookworm and an aging hippy free spirit, no longer seemed in firm possession of either identity. Instead, the woman that stood before him was a scarecrow, a patchwork of bits and pieces of what she'd once been, barely held together with memories and history, chewing gum and duct tape. She seemed to be experiencing something deeply profound, and confused as to how Lane couldn't be experiencing it too.

"Do *you* know who you are?" he asked her. "*What* you are?"

"Why are you speaking to me this way?"

"You would've hated it here," he said softly.

Claire looked around the dark room, as if she'd only just then realized where she was. She nodded. "I hate it everywhere."

"You used to be happy."

"So were you."

"I never stopped."

"Neither did I. Not voluntarily."

"I took it from you…"

"You stole it from both of us."

"It didn't have to be this way."

"Was it worth it?"

"I lost you—everything—over nothing."

"No, not nothing."

"Nothing, it was nothing, I—"

"Do you really think you get to escape it all so easily?"

"Is that what you think I'm doing?"

Expressionless and still, she stared at him with empty eyes.

"You want me to feel pain, is that it? Well I do, Claire. For

God's sake, agony is all I ever feel anymore. But tell me, where does forgiveness enter into this? Does it ever?"

"Forgiveness for what, Lane?" She licked her lips and sighed. "You were falsely accused, remember?" A shiver passed through him. "Temptation is a terrible thing."

"No," he said. "Everything that's terrible is in the shame, guilt and regret."

"They don't understand those things. They don't know what they are."

His pulse quickened. "Who are *they*?"

"Bad dreams." She looked away, as if something in the darkness had caught her attention. "They come true sometimes."

"That's it, isn't it?" Lane brought his hands to his head, ran them through his hair. They came back slick with perspiration. "I'm dreaming."

"You're awake."

"You're not real."

She reached out, let her fingertips gently brush the side of his face.

They were soft and warm, familiar. Nearly choking with emotion, his face contorted into a grimace as tears filled his eyes. "This isn't possible."

"Maybe everything's possible tonight."

Claire sunk down onto the edge of the bed, the darkness reclaiming most of her. "Sit with me awhile."

It took every bit of strength Lane had, but he slowly shook his head no. "Are you afraid of me, Lane?" she asked sadly.

"You're not my wife. You're not Claire. Not really."

She cocked her head, baffled. "Then who am I?"

The tears spilled free, ran the length of his cheeks. "I don't know."

"It doesn't go away, Lane, not until we release it."

"Am I in Hell?"

"There is no Hell. Only in us, we created it. Punishment and anger and revenge, greater powers have no use for any of that. God is love, forgiveness and transcendence. We're the ones who can't forgive, who need punishment and damnation, but we only damn ourselves, see? We *are* Hell."

"No. We're more than that. We have to be."

"It's within us, Lane. Maybe that's why we're so interesting."

Claire bowed her head as if suddenly overcome with prayer, and it was in that moment that Lane remembered *this* Claire. An old memory, from a time before things went bad, she looked and was dressed as she had been a few years prior while on vacation with him in the Florida Keys. A time of peace and togetherness, of love and joy neither would ever know again.

"They stole it," he said, trembling. "They crawled inside my head and stole that memory I have of you." He took a step back, away from her, his eyes rapidly scanning the shadows along the walls and ceiling. "They're watching us right now, aren't they?"

"I love you," she said.

"Still?"

"Always." This time it was Claire who cried. As a single tear ran across her face she seemed surprised, reached for it and scooped it up with a fingertip. Slowly, she brought it to her lips, tasted it. "They don't understand love either."

"Do they understand pain?" She blurred through his tears. Angrily, he wiped them away and addressed the darkness around them, screaming now. "Do you understand pain? Do you? Do you fucking understand that?"

He sunk to his knees, hands clutching his head as if to literally hold it together, and began to sob like he hadn't done since he was a child.

After a few moments he felt a hand gently moving through his hair, across the back of his neck and around to the side of his head. Gently, she pulled him closer and against him. Soft… warm…and yet…

Lane looked up at the woman standing over him.

No longer Claire, but Emma. Not a woman, but a girl.

Choking on the darkness, Lane managed to speak through the sobs, "No, you—you don't get to do this to me, you—you don't get to put her back in front of me then take her away like that. Please…Christ…*please…*"

"Get up and stop slobbering all over yourself like a little bitch." She moved away, toward the bed where Claire had just been sitting. "Try growing a set."

Lane struggled to his feet, wiping away the tears as he staggered after her. Taking hold of her wrist, he none-too-gently spun her back around to face him. "Where is she? Where is she, you little bitch! Where's my wife?"

Not even remotely intimidated, Emma smiled her crooked, cynical smile. "*Mister* B!" she said with mock astonishment, her icy blue eyes wide and alive. "Oh. My. God. You are *so* sexy when you're angry!"

He felt his free hand curl into a fist.

"Oooo, you gonna hit me now?" She easily pulled her wrist free of him and sauntered closer to the shadows by the bed. "Why not just fuck me and get it over with? Again."

Helplessly imprisoned in a tempest of his own guilt, fear and rage, Lane stood watching as Emma began to laugh. It was a cruel, heartless laugh that he did not remember her possessing.

"None of this was your fault, I…"

"I didn't have to turn your ass in," Emma said. "But it was so much fun watching you squirm and lie and try to find your way out of it. I figured then you might know how you made me feel."

"I never wanted to hurt you, Emma."

"Right back at you, Mr. B."

"Did you think I was in love with you, Emma? Is that what you thought?"

Her act vanished, and she stood before him more like the child she was than the temptress she so desperately wanted to be. "What difference does it make?" she asked in a soft, pained voice. "I was in love with you."

He took a tentative step toward her, his hands out before him like a traffic cop. "No, you—"

"Don't worry." Her expression turned to steel. "I don't love you anymore. I see you for what you really are. And you know what? *They* see it too."

It's the truth that scares you. It always has.

"I made a mistake, Emma, a horrible mistake. I'm so sorry."

She absently gave her forced cleavage a quick scratch. "Since we're just animals they don't really get it, you know? They're trying to understand."

Head spinning, Lane reached out and steadied himself against a wall he knew was there but could not see. "We're *human* animals."

"Problem is…they're neither."

"What's happening to me, Emma?"

She sat on the bed, in the exact spot where Claire had been sitting, and, folding one leg beneath her, left the other dangling off the edge. "OK, try to think of it this way. When we grab an animal in the wild for research purposes—a lion, let's say—and tag it, study it—whatever—do we explain ourselves to the lion? Even if we did, would the lion have any concept of what the fuck we were talking about? Through no fault of its own, the lion doesn't have the capability to even begin to understand what we're doing or why. It only knows it's afraid and wants to get the hell away from us. Just like you feel right now. Some like to laugh and point out how vastly superior another species would have to be in order to really exist and be interacting with us here on Earth. If they were so vastly superior, why would they have to abduct humans and perform crazy experiments on them? We're vastly superior to lions, so why do we do what we do? What people sometimes forget is that superiority doesn't rule out the possibility that such a species might be able to learn something from us, just as we do from the lion. They may not have a very good reason for what we perceive as fucking with us, but maybe they do. Same as the lion assumes we're there to do harm, maybe it's not always about help or harm at all. Maybe it's about something else entirely. Maybe it's bigger than all that. Think about the computers we have and all the things they can do. Now imagine what *theirs* might be capable of. Think about it. Who's to say what reality is, how it works or who controls it?"

She smiled at him. A genuine smile, real as Claire's fingertips brushing his face had been. Real as the darkness swirling around him like the living entity it was, and sacred as the evil and ancient eyes watching it all unravel.

Something clenched deep in his gut, and Lane doubled over and vomited a strange black, inky substance that splattered into a thick pool at his feet. Left lightheaded, he tried his best to focus on Emma…there…on the edge of the bed…just beyond his reach…

And then the cold…the snow…the wind…

It was not yet quite night, but no longer day. Twilight. It was twilight and somehow he was outside again, standing in deep snow, eyes trained on the outbuilding in the storm.

He felt someone touch him, a warm hand slip into his. But he was not afraid. He knew who it was. Looking to his left, he saw Claire standing there next to him. She should've been freezing but seemed completely unaffected by the storm. He reached back, cupped the side of her face and drew her to him. As they kissed, his eyes rolled shut and everything was right again.

But when he opened his eyes, she was gone.

He was alone. Again.

Turning back to the outbuilding, he watched and waited. He'd been mistaken. He was not alone. Not at all, as through the growing darkness and violent whirl of snow and ice, they came. From the forest, scurrying up and over the back of the outbuilding, swarming over the roof, scuttling and clicking and falling into the snow like a horde of angry insects, all spindly legs and arms and hideous heads and eyes, they rushed toward him in an impossible wave of madness and evil.

SIX

It's all there. Like a film playing in a theater in the round, the sounds and visions and senses happen all around him, assault him from every side, every angle. Exploding up out of the darkness like pillars of fire, things he cannot understand burst before him, space and time, stars and planets, endless expanses of night mixed with brilliant spires of colors and shapes he could've only imagined prior.

Helplessly, he waits and watches, his eyes burning as it all detonates and surrounds him, absorbs him until he is no longer a spectator, but a player, one with the universe igniting all around him.

Tumbling, falling slowly through darkness, he is unable to determine up or down as everything vanishes as quickly as it arrived, stranding him in an endless, starless night. Sucked into a vacuum of black silence, he slowly rotates and spins like an astronaut spiraling through space, his tether broken, alone in an unimaginable expanse of nothingness.

He thought he knew what it was to be alone, but now understands what it truly means. Hope is an illusion, a memory of something once possible that has been relegated to the realm of myth and broken promises whispered in the dark.

And just when he's sure the darkness will swallow him forever, it parts and night becomes day…

Rain sluices along a window facing the ocean. Sitting before the window is an old woman wrapped in a shawl. She gazes out at the ocean through the rain-blurred window, unaware that he is watching her. Her body is frail and her face is marked with the sorrow of a long and complicated life.

It isn't until he looks more closely that he realizes the woman is

Emma, the young girl replaced with an impossibly old woman. Gone is the tough-girl act. Her pain is not only real now, it is realized, forged by decades in the fire.

She does not see him—cannot see him—yet he senses she somehow knows he's there, even after all these years. Tears of blood spill from her eyes, smearing her ashen skin in swathes of dark crimson.

Running. He remembered running as hard and fast as he could. But the snow was too deep and thick, too difficult to negotiate, and he quickly became lost in the maelstrom of flakes, disoriented and overcome with horror and confusion. And then he was going down, being pulled down, dragged down into the snow. So cold and sharp, the icy snow scraping at his flesh as countless hands violently grabbed and yanked at him with their hideously inhuman fingers, the wind and a million evil whispers whirling, circling him like a pack of ravenous wolves until he was beneath the snow and all went dark and quiet.

Just as he was sure he'd died, Lane found himself free of his snowy grave somehow and moving through the front door to the house, Clyde and the others he'd seen earlier ahead of him and moving frantically to get inside as well. Despite his confusion, once inside, Lane closed the door and made sure it was locked behind him. As he stepped through the mudroom and into the kitchen, Clyde and Curly lowered Jed onto one of the chairs.

"How badly is he hurt?" he asked. "Not sure," Clyde said. Like the other two men, he looked panicked and frozen solid and was still covered in snow, his mustache flecked with ice. "He keeps coming in and out."

"You need to get him to a doctor."

"There isn't a doctor within ten miles of here."

"Let's get him in the other room then."

Lane led them into the den, where they placed Jed on the couch. Clyde leaned his rifle in the corner but Curly held his tight, gripping it with both hands now that he no longer had charge of Jed. One of his hands was bloodied and wrapped in a black bandana.

"Is your hand all right?" Lane asked.

Curly didn't answer, and as Clyde carefully lay Jed on his back, it became evident that the blood down the front of him was coming from a wound on his forehead, a gash two-to-three inches long. The wound was still bleeding, so Lane hurried to the bathroom and returned with a bottle of peroxide, tape, gauze and a hand towel.

Clyde took the towel, pressed it against Jed's forehead and applied pressure. The man jerked forward, as if to sit up, but Clyde gently pushed him back down. "Easy now," he said. "Got to get this bleeding stopped, OK?"

Jed's eyes opened but he didn't seem completely cognizant of where he was or what was happening. A few seconds later, he again drifted off into unconsciousness.

"What the hell happened?" Lane asked.

Curly Briggs, a stout and powerful looking man with broad shoulders, enormous hands, no neck, a perfectly bald dome and decidedly pig-like facial features, shook his head and shuffled away from the couch. He looked to be in shock, or perhaps frightened to the point where he'd begun to shut down as a result. Lane couldn't be sure which, but either way Curly clearly had no intention of answering him, so when he asked a second time, he addressed the question to Clyde.

Rather than answer, Clyde shot him a sideways glance then said, "Curly."

Lost in a tangle of memories and nightmares, the big man gave no response.

"Curly!"

This time he jumped, the spell broken. "Yeah?" he said restlessly.

"You get over by that front door and keep an eye out, you hear me?"

With a quick nod he strode back out through the kitchen to the mudroom.

"Clyde," Lane pressed, "*what* is going on?"

"Where's that shotgun you bought?"

"I..." Lane could've sworn he'd loaded it and left it against the kitchen table when he'd ventured into the bedroom, but he looked there, it was gone. "I'm not sure, I—I think the bedroom closet."

"Go get it and load it."

"Look, I need to know what's happening."

"I ever steered you wrong before?"

"I don't—what?"

"Since you've known me." Although Clyde looked terrified, his voice was composed and even, nearly monotone. "Have I ever steered you wrong?"

"No."

"Then trust me when I tell you it's important for you to listen real good." He pulled the towel away from Jed's wound, checked it then put it back and continued the pressure. "Go get the shotgun and load it. Right now." With visions of the strange footprints and the beings surging at him from the woods still in his head, Lane quickly made his way to the bedroom, found the shotgun at the rear of the closet and then the box of shells he'd purchased along with it in a drawer in the kitchen.

Curly stood by the front door staring out at the storm like a sentry made of stone. "Do you want to tend to that hand?" Lane asked.

Without turning around, Curly slowly shook his head in the negative. Lane returned to the den to find Clyde cleaning Jed's wound with peroxide. He stood there a moment then sighed, sat in the chair, loaded the shotgun with shaking hands and put the box of shells aside on the table. "We were running like madmen through the woods little over a mile from here," Clyde said, placing a square of gauze on the wound and taping it into place. "There was this low branch hanging down, big bastard, but Jed never saw it. Ran right into it at full speed, went down like he'd been shot. Thought it took his goddamn head off."

Lane forced a swallow. "Why were you running?"

The bleeding stopped and the wound dressed, Clyde rose from the couch and ran his hands through his long hair. "I wasn't totally honest with you before. We didn't go out to do any hunting, we parked the truck where we always do, followed the same path as usual, but this time we circled around and came up on Dwight Maynard's property from the back to see what was going on. Bunch of military guys were on the hill with the body, handling all sorts of fancy equipment and wearing Hazmat suits."

"Christ, that means there's hazardous materials or—"

"We stayed back behind the tree line," Clyde continued, "but even from there we could see that Dwight's body didn't look like before. It was...*changing.*"

"Changing how?"

"Decaying. Fast. We'd all seen the body a couple hours before and in that time Dwight went from looking like he was asleep to looking like he'd been dead and left to the elements for days." He shook his head, as if he still couldn't believe it. "They kept waving all these electronic wands and whatnot over him and tinkering with their equipment, but when they started cutting pieces of him off and putting them in little plastic baggies, we got the hell out of there."

"How'd you end up here?"

"We were making our way back when Chester—that's Curly's dog, best damn hunting dog I've ever seen—started acting strange. Sitting down, not wanting to move at first, and then wanting to run in the other direction. Curly tried to get him to mind, which was never a problem before, but Chester wouldn't listen. Finally he bit Curly just to get away from him, then turned and ran off. Didn't make any sense...until we saw them too." He looked at the floor, obviously disturbed as he relived what he and his friends had been through. "We all saw them at the same time, in a small clearing, about a mile in." Clyde looked to be slowly fracturing beneath the weight of what he'd witnessed, and was struggling to hang onto whatever scraps of sanity he could. "What I saw, what *we* saw, ain't possible. But they were there. Standing there, just...watching us." He grimaced like he was in pain. "Not men," he said, whispering now as if the words were too profane to be spoken any louder. He seemed to remember his rifle in the corner just then, and quickly snatched it up. "They weren't *human.*"

Fear rose from Lane's gut like bile bubbling up into the base of his throat. But even as his brain tried desperately to find an explanation and a way out of this nightmare, he knew Clyde was telling him the truth. "I saw them too."

"I know." Clyde's bloodshot eyes slowly closed. "And they saw you."

Something shifted deep inside Lane. He took a step back and looked to the floor. "Where's Vince?" he asked. "Where's my dog, he—"

Clyde's eyes opened. Empty sockets, dripping blood black as the night skulking in all around them. "Windows," he said, voice hollow and unfamiliar.

The three men—frozen and long-dead cadavers all—sprung into action, firing their weapons at the windows again and again as a wave of the beings attempted to flood through and into the house.

Moving on pure adrenaline and instinct, Lane racked the shotgun, spun and fired at the closest window, blowing one of the attackers back, out of the window and into the night in a spray of smoke, glass, snow and black blood.

The guns firing in such a small space were deafening, but they continued, Lane letting loose a primal scream of violence and madness while he racked the shotgun and fired again and again.

And when it was over, and all that remained were shattered windows, holes in the walls and a storm that was now gradually making its way inside, Lane realized he was standing by himself in the middle of the den, shells at his feet and a smoking shotgun clutched in his trembling hands.

He dropped the gun, heard it thud as it hit the floor. Then there was only the wind, building and howling and cutting him as bursts of snow blew in through the newly formed portals in the house.

As if in a trance, Lane walked to the mudroom, took up the ax from the woodbin then went out the front door and into the night, into the storm and into the snow, sinking nearly to his waist as he rounded the side of the house.

Lay down, Lane...lay down in the snow and sleep.

"Vince," he said softly. "Where are you?"

Everything will be all right if you just lay down in the snow and sleep.

"If you've hurt my dog I'll kill you. I'll kill every last one of you."

Something brushed his cheek. A tail.

He blinked. The flakes tickled his eyes. He watched them falling so gracefully, spiraling down from the heavens to cover him there in the drifting snow. Vince was there beside him. He couldn't quite see him—at least not clearly—but he could feel him. And just beyond where he lay, where he'd been caught and dragged down into the snow, from the very corner of his eye he saw them standing there, little hideous silhouettes in the night, silently watching with their horrible eyes.

His hand, frozen, split and raw, tightened on the ax handle.

He was cold…so very cold…and yet…it no longer seemed to matter.

SEVEN

Twilight.

From the heavens, something falls at dusk, descending to Earth. Something ancient. Something…alive.

When night comes the whispers grow louder, the feelings of unease more intense, sweeping across the open spaces and congested areas alike. Neither small towns nor cities are immune. The oceans and forests, the mountains and open plains, everything and everyone is infected as they slowly sweep across land and sea like dust devils, returned to reclaim what is theirs.

Not from outside, but from within.

A feeling…a strange sensation…that odd voice from the very back of your mind that promises despite what you know to be true and possible, this time the nightmare is real. Everything alive knows it, feels it, senses it and understands. Or soon will. Can you hear it? Are you listening? There's something here with us now, something close and growing stronger. At once alien and horrifically familiar, they listen. Watch. Wait.

But their time for waiting is over.

The feeling that a great change is coming, has come, and will soon reveal itself is overwhelming and slowly strangling the young and old, the rich and poor, cutting across every culture, every religion, encompassing every living thing, believer and nonbeliever, human and otherwise. And the future of mankind hangs in the balance like an invisible fog, a dark prophecy spun in the minds of wizards and sorcerers from long-forgotten ages of darkness, disease and death, awakening now to fulfill destinies chiseled in stone before the birth of Man.

As now it is Man who looks to the skies and watches. And waits.

Because the age of Man is dying, and with its death a door opens and a new age is ushered in across the globe, a time of something else.

Something other. Something close. The planet is no longer ours.

It never was.

Russell Brunel waited for a break in traffic then jogged across the street and joined Claire at a sidewalk café. Sitting alone in a summer dress and sipping a glass of wine, she looked as tired as he was, and despite the fact that it was a beautiful and sunny spring day, a dark cloud hung over them both.

Claire flashed an obligatory smile and shook Russell's big paw of a hand.

He plopped onto a chair across from her and straightened his thinning hair. "Good to see you, Claire."

"How've you been, Russell?" she asked flatly.

"Same. You?"

Her eyes were concealed behind dark sunglasses, but had he been able to see them he'd have known she wasn't looking at him but rather past him. "It is what it is, as they say." She shrugged.

A young waiter appeared and Russell ordered a beer.

"No news?" he asked a moment later.

Claire didn't answer right away. Instead, she sipped her wine. "I haven't heard from the police in weeks. I don't think they're even still looking. I mean, the way he left your apartment, writing all over the wall like some sort of maniac that he'd been 'taken.' They thought he was mentally ill right from the get-go, but even the search for someone suffering from mental illness only lasts so long."

Russell fidgeted in his chair. "But there's been no trace of him and—"

"There were no signs that he'd been kidnapped," she reminded him. "The lead detective told me it looked like he just walked out. Nothing was disturbed and they never found anything to indicate there had been any kind of foul play."

"Still gives me the creeps thinking about it. Coming home that day and finding the dog there all alone and that word written all over the walls. Jesus."

The waiter delivered his beer and moved away.

"It's time to come to grips with the fact that Lane's gone and he may never come back." Claire sighed heavily then took another sip of wine. "He was never the same after what happened in Maine. I knew nothing good would come of that." He chugged some beer then stifled a belch. "When I went up there I tried to get him to come back with me but he wasn't having it. Then winter hits and he almost freezes to death out there. People go crazy all the time in places like that. Long winter, all alone but for the dog, cabin fever sets in and who knows what might happen? Guy shoots the house up with a shotgun, goes out into the snow with his dog and lies down. Sound like someone in his right mind to you? Damn miracle those EMTs found him when they did. How he and Vince survived at all is a mystery. You heard the news reports, several locals died in that blizzard, froze to death out hunting or some nonsense."

"Lane was a grown man, Russell. He made his choices."

Russell looked down into his beer. "I did my best, Claire."

"I know you did."

"I tried to put him up, no pressure, helped him as best I could. I thought maybe in time he'd come around. He did his best too, he really did, but he was never the same. He just kept getting worse." He forced himself to look at her. "From the moment he lost you he was doomed."

She nodded, her lower lip trembling slightly. "So was I."

They were quite awhile. Sounds of traffic and passersby filled the silence.

"You should see that dog," Russell finally said. "He still sits all day and night waiting on him. Goes out to do his business, eats, sleeps in short little intervals and spends the rest of his time watching the door or looking out the windows. Almost like he's trying to bring Lane back by sheer will alone."

"After all this time you'll be keeping him I take it?"

"I've gotten attached to him. Not sure he's all that attached to me though. He's preoccupied. He's still waiting on Lane, I've never seen anything like it."

"It almost sounds like the dog knows something we don't."

"He does. Think about it. We never got the whole story behind Lane's breakdown in Maine. But Vince was there. He experienced it firsthand. He knows exactly what happened. We've only got pieces, fragments."

"Sometimes I wake up very late at night," she explained. "It's so quiet it doesn't seem real. I stare at the ceiling, the shadows, and sometimes think maybe Lane's in the room with me, watching. It's so strong sometimes, almost like if I just concentrated hard enough I'd be able to make him out in the dark. Then I wake up and realize it was only a dream. And for just a moment I think maybe everything was just one big nightmare, you know? Maybe if I reach over Lane will be lying there next to me. Maybe none of this ever happened at all." Claire polished off her wine and put the glass aside. "But it *has* happened, and we're all slaves to it. Wishing for Lane to somehow miraculously reappear—no matter how heartfelt it may be—won't make it happen."

He reached across the table and gave her hand a gentle pat. "We'll find him, Claire. Sooner or later I know we will. He's out there somewhere."

"Are you sure?"

Russell watched the street awhile. "Maybe he went back to the snow."

"What do you mean?"

"There were nights he told me they wanted him to go back to the snow, that everything would be all right if he just went back to the snow."

"He'd lost his mind, Russell. *They*? Who are *they*?"

"I don't know," he answered quietly. "But that dog does."

In the dark and cold, he saw it all, the past, present, the future.

Right there before him. So close and real he could reach out and touch it.

Touch *them.*

The dog was getting heavy. He'd gotten so big.

Lane put him down, and together they walked through the sea of flakes, deeper into the storm, the night, the snow. When Lane had found a good spot, he sat down then lay back, exhausted. As he sank into the drift, allowing the snow to take him, Vince curled up next to him.

With waves of drowsiness closing in, luring him closer to the darkness, Lane pretended that instead of being cradled by snow he was actually wrapped tightly in someone's loving arms. Oddly, it was not Claire he thought of, but Marla Snead in her filthy little room with the beads for a door and a large wooden crucifix propped in the corner.

How long's it been since somebody put their arms around you?

He imagined her there with him a moment, two lost and battered souls finding refuge, forgiveness, peace and tenderness in the endless ice and snow. Just like damnation, revenge and punishment, those things were inherently human, belonging to the realm of flesh rather than spirit.

His fantasies dissipated and only the howling wind remained, the falling snow and the creatures watching from the edges of night, the lords of twilight within each of us, hidden in a blizzard that had raged for eternity and would never, *could* never end.

It's within us, Lane. Maybe that's why we're so interesting.

As they crawled closer through the swirling snow, bringing with them salvation, damnation, transcendence or perhaps all three, Lane closed his eyes.

From somewhere far away, he saw Vince sitting in a window, waiting.

Who's to say what reality is… Waiting for him.

…how it works…

Something wet and heavy slapped his cheek.

…or who controls it?

Vince was licking his face, he was sure of it, and in that strange and harrowing moment, as splintered visions played out before his crippled mind's eye, Lane fell deeper into darkness, through all the horror, pain, fear and uncertainty into something else. Something extraordinary.

Puppy breath washed over him, and he felt himself smile.

ABOUT THE AUTHOR

Greg F. Gifune is a best-selling, internationally-published author of several acclaimed novels, novellas and two short story collections. Working predominantly in the horror and crime genres, Greg has been called, "The best writer of horror and thrillers at work today" by *New York Times* best-selling author Christopher Rice, "One of the best writers of his generation" by both *The Roswell Literary Review* and horror grandmaster Brian Keene, and "Among the finest dark suspense writers of our time" by legendary best-selling author Ed Gorman. Greg's work has been published all over the world, translated into several languages, received starred reviews from *Publishers Weekly, Library Journal, Kirkus* and others, is consistently praised by readers and critics alike, and has garnered attention from Hollywood. Two of his short stories, HOAX and FIRST IMPRESSIONS have been adapted to film, his novella MIDNIGHT GODS will soon be made into a feature film, and his novel CHILDREN OF CHAOS is under a development deal to be made into a television series. His novel THE BLEEDING SEASON, originally published in 2003, has been hailed as a classic in the horror genre and is considered to be one of the best horror/thriller novels of the decade. Greg resides in Massachusetts with his wife Carol, a few cats and a dog named Dozer. He can be reached online at:

gfgauthor@verizon.net or on Facebook and Twitter.

Visit his official site for updates and info at: https://gregfgifune.wordpress.com/

CROSSROAD
PRESS

www.ingramcontent.com/pod-product-compliance
Lightning Source LLC
Chambersburg PA
CBHW061238170626
46809CB00007B/2732

* 9 7 8 1 9 4 8 9 2 9 3 0 1 *